Garret Strong
The Invention of Teleportation
"Beam Me Up!"

Gary Cunitz

ISBN: 978-1-916954-28-1

Most facts in this book are based on actual and current fictional events.

Names have been change to protect the guilty.

Table of Contents

PROLOGUE

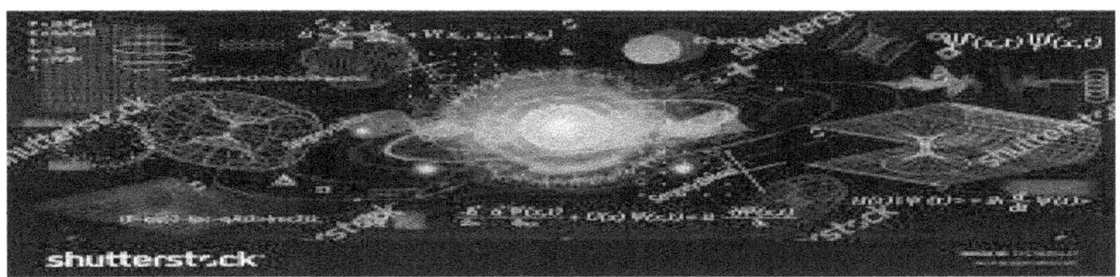

It is a world of technological advancements—powerful algorithms written and parsed in the language of a supercomputer. By the year 2030, it is believed that the world will witness incredible advancements in technology. It is believed that human-like A.I. will most likely be made possible through ultrahigh processing power of the computer. Software algorithms will be more complex and diverse for multiple inventions. Life will hover around these technologies. The effect of this, however, is that many people will be put out of work, which will result in devastating global economies.

But even so, it seems like scientists and engineers have unlocked the treasure to more groundbreaking inventions.

Garret Strong was regarded as one of the best students in an all boys' high school. The Dean of Discipline was an ex-marine drill instructor who pushed the boys' fitness and scholastics to another level. He made the competition tough. It soon became a case of survival of the fittest and the brightest. But even with the tight competition, Garret made it through as an honor science student. He was particularly good at physics, and would solve complicated calculations with ease.

Built like a NFL linebacker and standing at 6'4, Garret looked like a Greek idol. He had a kind of broadness right about his shoulders. His curly brown hair was at shoulder length. He had almond hazel eyes that looked quite mesmerizing when he fixed them on someone. His athletic talent and ruggedly-built frame got him a spot on–the football team. He grew into it so well that he earned the All-State MVP Football Star Award.

Garret's parents were in the military. His father was a Naval Aviator and his mother was a Naval Surgeon. But he was not pressured by them to join the Navy. With his academic records, his parents were convinced he would achieve great things in whatever field he decided to follow. However, Garret felt he could achieve more if he joined the Navy.

Ken Johnson, the Dean of Discipline at the school used his Marine Drill Instructor psychology on the boys. With a scowl to keep his face tight, he was a nightmare to the students. But somehow, Garret managed to find his soft spot. And sometimes, when they sat together at lunch, he would tell Garret about life in the military.

Mr. Barnes was Garret's chemistry teacher and best friend. He was a retired naval science officer – had his formal scientific training at the Naval Research Laboratory (NRL). And when Garret asked questions about his time at the navy, he had all the answers.

"I had my time experimenting, developing and testing powerful weapons," he had told him. "It's like a world of its own. There are rules – flout them and you get seriously punished. But it's not all about tough drilling and war, you know. You can be whatever you want to be. The NRL is studded with sophisticated research equipment that you need to become a great scientist…"

Garret's interest could be seen in his eyes as Mr. Barnes continued to tell him about the Navy and all that he could achieve there. He could already make a picture of the NRL in his mind. He could already see himself working on huge projects, either alone or with other science officers.

Yes, the words of Mr. Barnes sealed Garret's interest in the Navy. He was confident of the path he had chosen, and was glad that his parents did not force him into it.

And when Garret was through with high school, he was accepted into the Naval Academy. He majored in Laser Technology and Quantum Physics. The competition was fiercer in the Academy compared to high school. The Academy was a melting pot of diverse brilliant and talented young men. But Garret carried his brilliance along with him.

However, it was not an easy start at the academy. He might have been given an insight on how life was in the academy, but now he got to face them in reality. It was quite tough assimilating some of the courses taught at the academy. But to him, it was a challenge. And with time, everything fell in place. There was pride in wearing the Navel white uniform. It represented the heritage and honor of the Navy and the strength of the American military.

And for the extracurricular activities, Garret also played football for the Navy. He represented his academy in different competitions at different levels. Many eyes were on him, including those of principal officers. He became a popular name in the academy.

During summer vacations, Garret was enlisted among the 25 academy students that were invited to attend the Navy Seal Special Warfare training or better known as BUDS. It was a program only for the selected academy cadets. The Seals prepare and train the naval cadets from grinding through special weapons training to physical endurance test. These cadets are treated specially, and when fully inducted, get multiple deployments. It was an honor for Garret to train every summer as a Seal-Cadet. Being among these 25 students selected from hundreds kept him hard on his feet to remain at the top.

Indeed, Garret graduated at the top of his class. He was one of the best students. His principal officers evaluated Garret as 'outstanding and an over achiever' in the academy. He had his fair share of difficulty in the first few weeks at college, but he adapted quickly. Mr. Barnes ad Mr. Johnson was with him all the way.

Upon graduating from the Naval Academy Ensign Garret was assigned to the naval research lab (NRL) as a research scientist. With this assignment Garret is able to purse his master's degree in physics at Georgetown University while working at the NRL.

The Naval Research Laboratory (NRL) will help support Garret's master's thesis in Quantum Light Physics. The NRL, as he has seen, is equipped with the world's most sophisticated equipment, to foster the invention of new technologies, and the advancements of the already-existing ones.

There are various departments in the NRL: Atom and Quantum Sensing Department (AQS), Center for Disruptive Photonic Technology (CDPT) and Spin and Nanostructures Department, also called the Spintronics Department, Tactical Electronic Warfare (TEW). Garret works primarily in the Quantum science division, but shares time in the Atom and Quantum Sensing (AQS) Department.

The AQS Department is of fairly generous proportions. Just a distance from the door is the quantum computer. Standing across the walls are bioluminescence equipment, a noncontact optical inspection system, optical parametric device and Raman Spectrometer. There's a LaserBoxx LBX Series next to the spectrometer. A black hole is made on a piece of equipment that looks like a refrigerator. It stands between the LaserBoxx and a dark screen. The beam expanders and fiber optic sensors, even the micropositioner are all built onto the custom-built confocal quantum entanglement computer system that is near the north wall.

At the center of the room are working tables. It is where Garret physically analyzes the samples and reviews data on his super laptop. On the right is the control desk; on top of which are three supercomputers connected to the quantum computer processors. The computer analysis and detailing are done here.

Garret was up for the challenge. He was determined to break grounds in quantum physics. To have his name written amongst notable scientists like Albert Einstein, Max Planck, and the others. He believed he had all it took to reach the zenith of technological inventions, especially in the energy and engineering categories of quantum physics.

CHAPTER ONE:
THE BEGINNING

It is 9pm. The continuous beep from the indicator punctuates the silence in the NRL. There could be slow whirring in one of the equipment somewhere, but it is subsonic. Garret is standing in front of a custom-built Confocal Hadron Light Collider (CHLC) – the size of two large cargo vans. He is wearing an eye tracker. The sample he is working with a tiny piece of animal bone, has been placed on a mount that is placed on a retracting slide the size of a dinner plate. As Garret places the bone, it retracts into the large piece of equipment, and he watches carefully as the green laser beam passes through a laser scanner through the portal of the equipment.

It is Garret's first solo experiment and he's been at it for months. He wants to understand the interaction between a beam of light and an opaque body, and how this interaction can help in criminology. He has collected different samples from the Center for Disruptive Photonic Technology—a department in the NRL. Each of these samples, like graphite, metal, and some bio-samples, gave different readings as regards the aim of the experiment. But the red outs were inconclusive. Now Garret works with a fragment of bone in hopes that the data provided will lead him to the next phase of the experiment.

The light is collected and analyzed in a Photon Counter surrounded by a number of the CMOS sensors within the CHLC.

Garret remains undistracted, seemingly ready to direct the laser beam back to position if it is diffracted.

Apparently satisfied with what he is seeing and the data on his computer, Garret moves over to the quantum computer by a corner of the lab. It is a giant piece of equipment, with complicated twists and turns of cables and coils within a large silver cylinder within it.

Upon analysis of the images on the computer, Garret discovers streaks of light like meteor shower. Some of these streaks pass through the sample – others go halfway through, while others rebound and circle the specimen. His eyebrows crinkle with surprise. He used a single molecule of the sample - how is it that the result seems like he used a bio sample the size of the little finger? He was expecting a single streak of light, considering how meticulous he had been so far.

Garret has his hand across his jaw, propped up on his elbow as he clicks on different icons on the screen. The multiple streaks appear to be the problem in his research. If he can get a single streak from a single photon and a single molecule, maybe the analysis and results will take him through the next step.

But perhaps if he strengthened the beam of light hitting the sample, he will get a single streak. He will have to make sure there are no diffractions – not even in the infinitesimal – and that means bringing the laser to the most direct and precise focus on a point on the sample. That is it! That must be it, he thinks.

He gets off the chair, enthusiastic to try out his theory. He returns to the confocal collider.

The sample is placed on the slide and focused against the screen. Garret turns up the laser again. The tiny fiber is between 1000 and 1500nm. With the accessories attached to the laser system, Garret focuses the beam on the sample. He has put the eye tracker back on. Now he watches the result of the interaction on the screen.

But suddenly, the indicator begins to beep faster. Garret shoots his eyes at the equipment that resembles an amplifier on a table near the quantum computer. Something is not right. He removes the eye tracker and dashes toward the indicator.

He turns the knobs and dials on the control panel. The beep continues, louder and faster. There is a sizzling sound from the confocal collider. It is loud. The whole set-up is shuddering violently. Garret quickly strides toward it, having realized that the problem is obviously because he turned up the frequency of the laser.

The lights in the department are starting to flicker. There are more sizzling sounds coming from nearly every piece of equipment in the department. The quantum computer is vibrating and giving off tiny sparks. Emergency red lights in the ceiling begin spinning activating a load ring alarm in the entire building.

Garret is a few feet away from the set-up when it suddenly explodes. There are tiny sparks shooting in every direction with what appears to a small light tornado. Every material that is made of glass begins to shatter, sending shards of it into the air. A wave erupts in the confocal collider and bursts into a wide-spread ripple. Garret is thrown backward with the force and slammed against the LaserBoxx Series. Perhaps it would have been more devastating if he had landed on the quantum computer, which now emits sparks in different directions. It is time to get out of here.

Garret manages to find his feet on the ground. He glances through the broken door. It dawns on him that the destruction is not only happening in the AQS department but the whole of the NRL. The lights are flickering; alarms are ringing – the bare bulbs are shattering in the wave traveling across every corner of the laboratory. Alarms are deafening. Science officers are scampering about, looking for a way to stop what is about to unfold. They are trying to secure as many sensitive materials as they can before they run out of the laboratories.

"What are you doing there, Garret? The lab's gonna blow up," one of the science officers yells at him.

Garret knows that this is true. The lab is all about light and glass and both electric and magnetic fields - there's also the presence of radioactivity. With these sparks and ripples of waves, the whole NRL going up in flames is inevitable.

But as Garret stumbles backward toward the exit, he notices something: the laser beam has suddenly become a bit brighter and is swirling light a dust devil with green and white light. The space between his brows snaps shut with surprise. Questions are raised in his mind as to what he has just seen: could it be that the electrical surge turned up the frequency of the laser beam? Is the beam somehow reacting to the intense heat? The latter is almost impossible. Garret has a feeling that something has undeniably occurred – a reaction.

Risking the explosions, he gets closer to the portal of the confocal collider. The sparks are everywhere. The whole lab is like a ticking time bomb – just the right moment and everything and everyone will be reduced to fragments. Garret coughs as he moves closer to the portal. The cloud of smoke that is starting to gather is choking him. He puts on the eye tracker hoping to discover something extraordinary.

And yes, he does. The light is stronger before reaching the screen and Photon Counter because the single molecule of bone is no longer in its path. It is latched on the screen. And there's a hole at the point where the laser meets the screen. Garret thought at first that it could be due to the heat and perhaps radioactivity going on as the lab explodes – or perhaps a shard of glass must have broken the screen. But he is shocked to realize that the point is not melting away, if it is as a result of the heat or radioactivity.

On a closer look, Garret discovers that the point is getting wider, and the sample is no longer latched on it. The specimen starts to float. The part of the screen appears like it's disappearing as it gets wider.

Garret observes that before it vanishes in the light tornado. There's some sort of agitation within the glass as it glows green and white, and then it all disappeared. Gone! Vanished into thin air……

While Garret stands astonished. The whole Confocal Hadron Light Collider is ablaze.

"Get outta there, Garret. Now!" a voice orders from behind. Suddenly the fire suppression system activates and all the fire sprinklers are gushing down water from the ceiling.

Whether it is from his superior or not, Garret knows it is indeed time to leave. The lab is just a moment away from catching on fire or being flooded. Garret finally stumbles out through the exit grabbing his laptop from the side table, with half his mind pondering over what he has just witnessed. Now most parts of the NRL lab is being destroyed – the pieces of equipment and anyone who is so unfortunate to play the hero. The firefighters have arrived and are doing all they can to stop the fire from spreading – for if it is not brought under control fast enough, the whole NRL building will be destroyed. Garret may have witnessed something he thinks is spectacular, but he will have his superiors to face when morning comes, and he knows this.

***

The disciplinary committee did not convene in the morning. The accident was still under investigation at the time. There are a lot of damages to the building and equipment. And although many fingers point at Garret, the head of the NRL, acting according to the Naval Protocol, decided that they carry out a deep investigation first.

Five days later at 1600 hours, Garret is summoned to the Inspector General's building adjacent to the courthouse. He knows it is time to face some consequences. The events of last week are still a marvel in his eyes. All through his time at college, working with different pieces of equipment, he has never witnessed a laser beam interacting with a specimen and then disappears. And if it actually disappeared, then to where? But maybe he has to put his mind to where he's been summoned – he could have a lot more to face than he thinks.

And now, Garret stands in a hall filled with portraits hanging on the wall of past Admirals and Commanders of the Navy. Garret enters what is set up as a military courtroom. There are chairs behind a long table. Sitting in front of the long table and chairs is a large podium in which Michael Watt, the head of the NRL and an admiral himself along with other high-ranking naval officers are sitting looking down at Garret. All the officers are between the ages of 50 and 60, dressed in their star-spangled white uniforms with medals dangling off of their chests. Garret can almost see his punishment by the looks on their faces.

"Ensign Garret Strong, I believe you know why you have been summoned here?" Michael questions.

"Yes sir," Garret replies.

He heard the whispers – in the past few days he heard the rumors – all before now. He knows it is pointless denying it.

"For the benefit of doubt, I will state it clear: that last week, at 2100 hours, the NRL lab was subjected to destruction as never seen before – and that at this time, you were carrying out an experiment in the Atom and Quantum Sensing Department. Am I correct?"

"Yes sir."

"And this ultimately incriminates you as the cause of the destruction…"

Admiral Michael is quiet and shuffling through the papers in front of him. He seems to be waiting for Garret to affirm to his last statement, but Garret does not. He knows he is guilty, but admitting it expressly is not right. After all, someone else could be working in one of the other departments at that time too.

"We've carried out our preliminary and very extensive investigation and have discovered that the explosions emanated from the department you were working in. The security footage and other pieces of evidence that we gathered lend credence to this fact. You were experimenting with laser beams and biological samples. Analyses reveal that you may have manipulated the strength of the beams intensity that it interfered with the connections in the lab, which ultimately gave rise to the fire and destruction to half of the NRL facility. What do you have to say about this?"

"The analyses are true, sir. I was close to achieving the aim of my experiment. And so I think that in the process, I may have turned up the laser beam to a point it interfered and caused a meltdown and overloaded the other systems in the lab."

"Now are you aware that this carless act of yours caused the destruction of powerful and sensitive pieces of equipment in the lab, and caused several degrees of injury to a number of officers?" Not to mention the destruction of millions of dollars in sensitive lab equipment."

"I am aware, sir, and I take full responsibility for my actions."

Admiral Michael shuffles through the papers again. The last officer on his right passes another piece of paper to him across the table. With the paper in his hand, he clears his throat and continues.

"Having carried out an extensive investigation, you, Ensign Garret Strong have been found guilty of breaching the Naval Protocol. This protocol states that all experiments must be carried out within the limits and specifications of the lab. Your actions have not only caused the destruction of the Naval Research Laboratory but have costs the taxpayers millions of dollars. Therefore, following the protocol guiding such a military felony, you are hereby comprehensively immediately dismissed from the Navy. This means that all military benefits that you were entitled to are withdrawn, and all back pay is renounced as well – all with immediate effect. This punishment cannot be appealed. You have 3 hours to surrender every property of the Navy that is in your possession and leave the premises. You will be regarded as a spy if you are found within the premises after 3 hours and will be treated as such. You are lucky that you're not spending years of imprisonment. Because of your family's military service, we as the court are being very lenient with you."

Garret is silent for a while. His feet are frozen – his knees wobbling. He feels the punishment is too harsh. From what he knows, a comprehensive dismissal for such misdemeanor is a dishonorable discharge. He can already tell how unfairly he's been treated. He is convinced that this is not a protocol guiding his offense but a decision by blind disciplinary board a haste in judgment to appease higher ranking government officials pushing their political clout. But he also knows it is pointless protesting, neither can he plead for clemency. A soldier never asks for mercy! And with that, he tries to keep a calm disposition.

"Thank you, SIR," he says.

He manages to throw a salute even when his arms are heavy with sadness.

"Dismissed and good luck," the man next to Admiral Michael orders.

With face flushed, Garret turns and marches toward the door, from whence he will go to the lodge and do as he's been instructed. He will say goodbye to his friends with a sad look on his face. He's not really had a close friend here in the Navy. He's kept it casual, focusing all of his time and effort on his experiments. And then he will pack up his personal belongings and leave the premises – he will leave the place he's dreamt to be in all his life.

Being dishonorably discharged makes Garret seem like a disappointment, seeing how far his parents have gone in the Navy. In fact, at the moment, he sees himself as one. But perhaps there is more to explore as a civilian. Perhaps being a civilian will grant him greater freedom and allow him to experiment without boundaries, to reach the peak of his science career – and that, he is about to find out.

CHAPTER TWO:
MY MENTOR

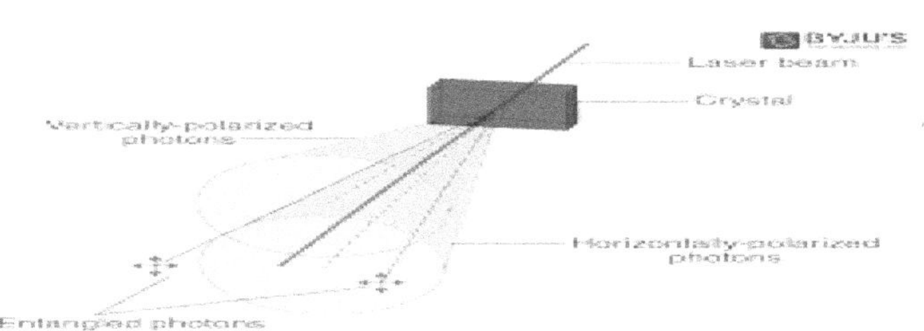

Shifting to the civilian life was an easy transition for Garret. It is not an entirely new experience for him after all. He's been in the Navy, both as a student and as an officer for years. And that has shaped his life in the military ways with discipline and ethics. However, at this point, he is more concerned with getting back to his experiment.

It's been a week since he was dismissed from the Navy, and his thoughts have been more inclined at what he saw in the portal of the Confocal Hadron Light Collider (CHLC). He has not stopped wondering what it means. He wants to get back to the laboratory as quickly as possible, and for that, there's only one person he can call – his best friend, and old High School science teacher, Mr. Barnes…

"That was a harsh treatment from your superiors, boy," Mr. Barnes comments after Garret had told him everything.

Mr. Barnes is of a regular height and physique, and walks with a slight limp and speaks with a Tennessee draw. He's got a pair of beady eyes that Garret thinks see a possibility where there seems to be none. He's been a father figure to Garret – that nerdy kid, from grade one. Garret has nothing but admiration for him, and the love of a friend. He calls him 'Barny', and Mr. Barnes thinks it's cool. He says the name makes him appear younger than his age, and grants him a better relationship with his students.

Now they both sit at the bartender's counter with a glass of tequila next to each of them. They talk in slow measured cadences so as not to give out information even to the bartender standing a few feet away behind the counter.

"Yeah, but I didn't have a choice," Garret replies. "I guess I deserved it…"

"No, you didn't, Mr. Barnes snaps. "A comprehensive dismissal is too harsh a punishment. For what? Blowing up the laboratory which ultimately injured your fellow officers? Experiments can go horribly wrong. It's normal. It's been like that even in the time of Einstein. We just keep trying until we achieve our goal."

Garret sips on his tequila and gently lays the glass on the counter.

"There's something else, Barny," he says and adjusts his bottom on the chair. "While the explosions were going on, I think I may have witnessed something strange."

"What's that?" Barny takes up his glass and sips his tequila looking at Garret.

"Before I escaped out of the burning lab, I observed that my working sample was no longer on the plate," Garret answers. "I got closer to the Confocal Hadron Light Collider portal and discovered that the laser light was reacting somehow with the sample. And as I watched, the sample just disappeared."

"I don't understand – is that some kind of laser breakdown or what?"

"No, it's not. And you know what: the reaction within the molecules appears to have spread wider before it disappeared…"

"That's strange!"

"Unfortunately, I didn't get to see everything as the equipment crashed. But I can tell something extraordinary happened."

Barny is silent for a while as Garret sips from his glass again.

"Don't you think that could have been as a result of you turning up the frequency of the laser? We're talking about a beam of light stronger than a regular light, one powerful enough to cause disruptions in the molecular level of most substances."

"Turning up the frequency of the laser could have contributed to what I saw, but I tell you, it is more than an ordinary disruption."

"What is your theory then?"

Garret takes a breath and reclines on the back of the bar stool, resting half his right arm on the counter, and gazing rather hopelessly at Barny.

"I honestly don't have any at this point…"

"Or maybe you think it might sound foolish if you say it," Barny cuts in.

The corners of Garret's mouth stretch into a smile. He knows Barny has him right at the spot. How can he understand him so well? It's as if he can read his mind.

"Come on, boy, I've known you your entire life. I can tell when you have something going on in that little head of yours. Out with it: what do you think?"

Garret clears his throat and sits up again.

"Yeah, you got me. Well, I know it's gonna sound weird but I think it could be some sort of teleportation induced by the laser light turning into a funnel just like a mini-light-tornado. I mean, that's been the only thought on my mind ever since I saw it."

"And why do you think it could be teleportation?"

"I'm not sure, but the fact that the sample disappeared completely from the plate and the part of the mini-tornado spinning around the sample, I feel it has to do with teleportation. 'Cause I keep asking myself: where did it go? I literally saw the sample disappear; I watched it hover and then disappear before my very eyes. I saw the interaction – I saw the light swirling around the specimen. It was dispersed into different colors, green and white mini-tornado. The faster the mini-tornado the lighter and transparent the specimen became, then it just vanished.

"When I got home I diligently reviewed the computer data on my laptop. Surprisingly, the computer information led to Einstein's formula of relativity theory to quantum teleportation, you know the EPR paradox."

Barny has been looking at Garret all the while he talked, and all he can see is that brilliant little boy he taught in school.

"I think you've got yourself a major experiment, boy. You could be at the verge of discovering the science of teleportation and proving Einstein theory. Who knows, it could apply to humans as well. I do not want to begin to imagine what the world will be like if it becomes successful, whether it can teleport humans or not. This could be nature's compensation for your unfair dismissal from the Navy."

"That's true. But at this point, I barely even know from where to start. I don't have a lab I am working in – I mean, no job. I don't even have the human and financial resources to set up my own lab. It's gonna cost a lot of money, you know."

Barny does not reply to that – instead, he grabs his glass and sips on the tequila. Garret glances at the bartender who's attending to a customer at the far end of the counter, and then brings his eyes on Barny again.

"Um, Barny, I was thinking if I could work in your lab. Do you mind?"

Barny drinks from his glass again and smacks his lips.

"Thought you'd never ask, boy…"

Garret smiles. He knows Barny will easily accept him in his lab – he doesn't even have to ask. But he was unsure he would agree, having been told about what happened in the NRL lab. Barny knew he was thinking about it, and was waiting for him to say something.

"Of course you could," Barny adds. "But I'll tell you that my laboratory is not as sophisticated as the NRL. We not only carry out experiments in the lab, we also fix faulty pieces of lab equipment that has expired manufactures warranties. To carry out this major experiment of yours, you will need powerful equipment of all sorts. I don't think my laboratory supports that for now. So we will scout for these pieces of equipment the best ways we know. You understand?" "There may be equipment that we need in the used market. The new equipment is overpriced."

"Thank you so much for the offer, Barny. I…"

"Shut up and have a drink, boy."

Garret laughs again. That is typical of Barny, he knows.

Barny drains what is left in his glass and mops the corners of his mouth with his handkerchief?

"You leaving with me or you wanna have some more (gesturing at the bar filled with assorted tequilas)?"

"I don't wanna have some more, but I don't wanna leave now either. Just want to sit here for a while – getting used to this kinda life, you know, the civilian life" Garret replies with a light smile.

"All right. You know where the laboratory is. I'll see you tomorrow morning in the lab. Get some rest."

"I will. Thank you."

Barny pats Garret's shoulder and heads toward the door. Garret sips gently on his tequila. He is glad that he's let it out to someone who believes in him. Even to him, the theory of teleportation had seemed crazy. But he couldn't think of anything else. It was the only explanation for what he saw. It is quite clear that Mr. Barnes thinks the same way too, even though he did not see the reaction. And right now, all there is to it is finding the necessary equipment for the experiment.

Not too long after Mr. Barnes left, Garret decides it's time to leave too. He pushes the money for the drinks across the table to the bartender.

"Keep the change," he says.

By the time the bartender replies with a 'thank you', he is already close to the door. For someone that wants to acquire expensive pieces of equipment, maybe he shouldn't be giving tips. Maybe Barny would have told him this if he was here – or maybe he would have been reminded that generosity is a part of Garret, having known him since elementary school.

Garret ambles along the pedestrian walkway, with his hands in his pocket. There's a bustling of city life – cars and other pedestrians going about their business. But even with these, Garret is preoccupied with the thoughts of how to find the pieces of equipment he needs. The enthusiasm in him to get back to his experiments burns like fire. Just like Barny said, a successful experiment could be nature's way of compensating him for the unfair treatment he got from his seniors at the Navy. The possibility of success is already taking up spaces in his head.

As Garret ambles along the road, a black SUV cruises behind him. He did not notice it at first. But as the SUV slowly swishes past him, the back window is down. Garret spots a man in the car glaring at him. His countenance darkens at once, perhaps to fend off the man's scowling look, but he keeps his eyes at Garret. Those dark eyes – that disfigured nose – that bearded face – he has not seen them before. He wonders who this man is and why he is all eyes on him.

And just like that, the man's face is hidden behind the tinted window as it is raised. The car accelerates faster. Now Garret is left with questions as to the identity of the man – or could the Navy be keeping tabs on him? He doesn't think that's right. And he's quite sure he has not stepped on the wrong toes since he was reduced to a civilian. He has a feeling their paths will cross again.

The taxi pulls over in front of Garret's house. The door slams shut as he steps out. He looks around to make sure no car has pulled over somewhere too. Since the incident with the man in the SUV, he has been extra cautious about his surroundings. And as his taxi drives away, he walks to his townhouse.

It is a small townhouse in Washington DC – a five-minute walk to Georgetown University. There are flowers in front of it, and lawns on both sides, between which is a pathway that leads to the door. Garret makes his way through this pathway, utterly suspicious of his environment. He suddenly feels like he is being watched – like there's a secret camera somewhere.

Even when he is inside the townhouse, that feeling lingers. He stands at the center of the sitting room and looks around the house. Apparently not satisfied, he marches into the rooms and kitchen and even the bathrooms, and then back to the sitting room. At this time, his paranoia has begun to fade. He is getting more comfortable.

The interior of the townhouse is casually furnished – couches arranged in a semicircle, a table at the center, a large TV on the wall, sound system just below the TV, and a chandelier hanging down the form the ceiling. The extension on his right is the dining room – through it is a door leading to the two rooms available in the townhouse.

Garret's laptop is his comfort pillow. His feet thud lightly against the floorboards as he marches to his room, not failing to glance outside through the window.

In a short time, he returns to the sitting room, looks through the window again and then settles himself on the couch. He opens his laptop and presses the power button. Only one thought sits in his mind right now: to make research on places he can buy the pieces of equipment he needs for his experiments. He knows that some of these things can be found on the used or black market sites. And if that is true, they will be affordable to him. But at the same time, he is not sure he will find information about those black markets online.

Even if his research gives him the information he wants, he will still need other powerful equipment from top laboratories, not only in the country, but around the world. First things first: he will think about that later. For now, he has to find out how to get equipment on the used market.

His research takes him through the whole night. And just as he feared there was no descent used lab equipment. His next target is the black market. With hours of searching he could not find legit information about how to reach the black market. It seems like people are afraid to give out such information. While he was in a community marketplace blog, he commented:

"Does anyone here know where I can buy scientific research equipment at affordable prices?"

The only reply he got was:

"Wrong place, bruh; look elsewhere."

This comment was from an anonymous person who blocked his identity so people could not reach him – maybe people like Garret who is in dire need of information.

He will have to continue his work at Barnes' laboratory, even though it will not be on a large scale like in the NRL. Through the night, he continues to review the notes and formulas on his laptop. For Barnes' lab, he needs to get ready for tomorrow.

***

The building is stretched across a land about the size of a lawn tennis court. It is located along Road 75, toward the east of Washington DC. Across the steel board is the name 'BARNES' LABORATORY FOR QUANTUM PHYSICS'. Garret can count the number of windows across the walls. But it is normal for a quantum laboratory. It is to prevent too much ultra violet light from entering the lab and destroying some of the samples and even the equipment. There are cars and robotic trolleys at different locations in the premises. Garret has been here before – but that was during his high school years. Being here now, he feels like a couple of things have changed. Like the name on the steel board – it was not as big as it is now, and the robotic trolleys too – they weren't there before.

Back then, Garret had been left to wonder why a chemistry teacher would own a physics lab instead of a chemistry lab – not just a high school physics lab, but one designed for college students and post graduates.

"I love the sciences. I was an honor student in my college where I studied Quantum Physics just like you hope to. I love optics and the related fields. At the same time, I love teaching too. I love sharing my knowledge of science with the future generations. And so I decided to teach chemistry part time at high school but continue with what I studied in college and in the Navy at the NRL. So in a way, teaching chemistry at high school is for my love for teaching and for the students, and owning a quantum laboratory is for my personal life as a physicist."

This explanation had solved the riddle in Garret's mind. But till now, he still wonders how Mr. Barnes manages to keep up with both aspects of his life.

He has called Barny on the phone. In his black trouser and pinstripe shirt, he makes his way to the door.

As he walks through the door, his nose flares to the smell of a regular compound he always finds in the Center for Disruptive Photonic Technology in the NRL – tri-n-octylphosphine. It is one of the solvents used in the synthesis of Ternary Quantum Dots.

"Get over here, boy!" Barny is standing at the front counter talking to the receptionist as he calls Garret's name when he enters the front door.

Garret looks in his direction and walks toward him. His eyes feast on the pieces of equipment thru the glass off the lobby: there are the regular ones like the optical parametric device, beam expanders, even the quantum computer and Parallelograph, some colloidal nanocrystals in a glass case, some semiconductors displayed on a silver table – other equipment for electron beam lithography, molecular beam epitaxy, X-ray lithography and microwave radiation – there's also the Polarizable Continuum Model (PCM), CMOS equipment and a lot more that he could see.

The laboratory is divided into departments by transparent glass walls, and most of the pieces of equipment Garret see are sectioned into each of the departments as he walks with Barney thru the lab. It may not be as large as the NRL, and may not possess the same sophisticated equipment, but Garret is grateful to be here. There's already a feeling of satisfaction and optimism in him that he will achieve his aim in this lab.

Barny and Garret approach two other men dressed in white lab coats. They are standing next to an optical testing system.

"Hey George and Daniel, this is Garret," Barny makes a casual introduction. "He's from the Naval Research Laboratory. He'll be working with us from now on. And Garret (turning), these (gesturing) are the scientific engineers here – George and Daniel. They are good at what they do. Whatever device you want customized; they'll take care of it – like the Confocal Hadron Light Collider."

"Straight off to quantum research, huh?" George cuts in.

"Exactly!"

Garret and Daniel smile.

"Nice to have you here, man," Daniel says.

"Same here. We got a lot of ground-breaking technologies to invent," Garret replies.

"That's the spirit!" George intones vocally.

Mr. Barnes taps lightly on the optical system and turns to Garret:

"Come on, boy – let me show you around. (Turning to the engineers) You two, get on with this. We must have it fixed as soon as possible."

"All right, sir…"

Barny leads Garret out of the research lab toward other parts of the lab.

"What is wrong with the system?" Garret inquires.

He already takes a shine to how friendly George and Daniel are and hopes to work with them soon enough.

"There's an issue in the inner core, and that affected the entire system and its output. It belongs to J & J Labs. We hope to fix and return it in two days – it's one day gone already…"

Barny takes Garret around the lab, showing him the various departments. Garret already knows his department - the one that has the quantum computer sectioned to it. This lab will be his new home. There is still a lot to learn, and he believes he will gain greater knowledge here.

"Garret, your new home.... Barnes' Laboratory for Quantum Physics..."

CHAPTER THREE:
THE PAST

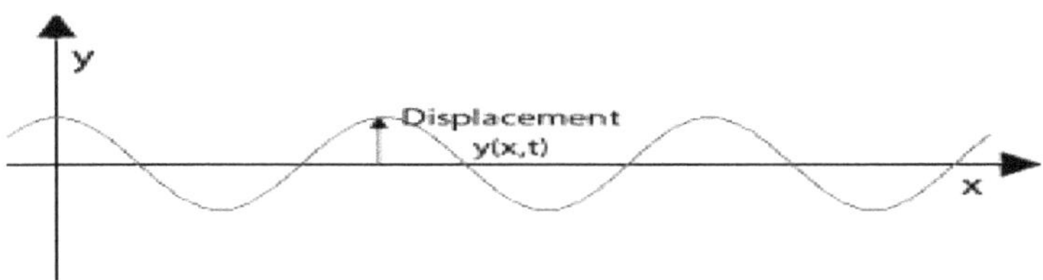

It is Garret's second day at Barnes' laboratory. He's asked George and Daniel to assemble a custom Confocal Hadron Light Collider for him. Meanwhile, he's been working with other equipment in the lab. He's been trying to understand why his experiment at the NRL went horribly wrong. The beam expander, the micropositioner, and other equipment he used in the experiment - he has analyzed every one of these to decipher what went wrong. And until George and Daniel complete the Confocal Hadron Light Collider (CHLC), it will be more theoretical. He will however, continue to work in other aspects of the lab while he waits.

This morning, Garret is summoned to Barny's office. He sits at the table as Barny writes on a piece of paper in a file. There's a LaserBoxx Series, Dialoid Spectrometer and optical screens, amongst others in the office.

Barny soon finishes what he is writing and looks up:

"As you know, we were able to fix the optical laser system. Now it's time to deliver it to the J & J Labs. I want you to lead the delivery and installation as well. George will go with you to assist you. Any questions?"

"Nope, Barny."

"Good. You should be on your way in the next 15 minutes. Let's go get the equipment loaded onto the flatbed truck..."

***

"So what's it like in the Navy?" George asks as they drive to J & J Labs.

He's on the steering wheel, feeling quite enthusiastic. Garret can already tell he has interest in joining a big laboratory like the NRL. But who wouldn't? The NRL is a dream lab to many research scientist and engineers - George is only one of many.

"It's a great place," Garret answers. "I'll admit they have state-of-the-art equipment, but our lab measures up, trust me."

"Can one apply for a space there?"

"Nah, it's for the military officers only who are trained in the science field. It's not all about war and drilling, you know…"

The corner of Garret's mouth rises into a side smile. He remembers those words from Ken, his Dean of discipline back in high school.

"You were a student there, right?" George asks.

"Yes. So I easily moved to the lab when I graduated the academy. But hey, it's not as great as you think. There are also the down sides. The lab is operated on strict Naval protocols - break any of them and you will be severely punished - you might even be dismissed. But here at Barnes', you're not limited. You can do whatever you want."

George is silent, but only for a moment. He glances at Garret.

"Breaking the protocols and getting dismissed - I guess that was what happened to you."

Garret sighs and adjusts his seatbelt.

"Not really..."

It wouldn't make sense if he told George what happened, no matter how close it seems like they have become. He's an enthusiast and Garret does not trust what he will do with his story if he shared it with him.

Finally, the vehicle pulls over in front of the building. It is the J & J Labs inscribed on the glass across the top of the building.

Garret steps out of the truck and scans the environment. There are cars parked around and robotic trolleys just like at Barnes'. But one of the cars catches his attention. It is an SUV, resembling the one that drove past him the other day, with the mysterious man glaring at him from it. Although Garret is not sure of his thoughts, he is wary of his environment. However, there's a second thought that says: 'what if this is not the same SUV?' Garret settles his mind on this - even so, his eyes can't stop trying to reach everywhere.

As soon as the vehicle came to a stop, two men wearing orange coveralls, come through the thick steel door of the building by the loading dock - one of them is driving a forklift. It's obvious they have been waiting for the delivery.

"Yo, what's up man?" one of them hails.

"We good," George replies.

"Got a new man?"

They all glance at Garret.

"Fresh from the Naval Research Laboratory," George answers proudly.

"Oh man, we got Einstein in our midst. Welcome man..."

They both shake hands with Garret who isn't okay with George telling them where he came from. But he tries to keep a cheerful face.

"All right, guys, let's get this stuff out and go have it installed," the other man in the orange coverall urges them.

The optic laser system is carefully brought down from the truck. It's so clean it left the men gushing.

"Whoa, you got some A-grade system right here. Chief scientists will be glad to see this," one comments.

"For real," the other replies.

"Come on, guys, we haven't got all day," George chivvies them.

The system is loaded onto the forklift and driven toward the lab. Garret still has his eyes everywhere. The longer he is here, the more vulnerable he feels. But this is his first official assignment. He must see to it that it is successfully completed.

The door of the lab opens and the men drive through. Immediately Garret comes through, his eyes fall on the same man that has kept him wary of even his own house since the incident along the road. He is standing with another man wearing a white lab coat somewhere at the end of the lab.

The man's eyes and those of Garret's met as soon as the door opened, but he quickly looked away this time as though he was avoiding him.

The man in the white coat breaks off and walks toward Garret and the others. He is most likely in his early 60s in Garret's judgment at first glance. Garret himself has hardly taken his eyes away from the other man who is still in position. He barely glances at Garret.

"Hello George," the man in the white coat greets.

"Hi Chief. We got your system looking all new."

The Chief Scientist smiles and checks out the optical laser system.

"Thank you. And I see you got a new man," he replies.

"Yeah, from the Naval Research Laboratory." George winks at Garret who manages to force a light smile.

"Oh really - that's interesting."

Chief turns to Garret.

"Hello, everyone calls me Chief," he greets and shakes hands with him. "I have a friend that works in the NRL. He is one brilliant scientist. What department were you in?"

"The Atom and Quantum Department."

"Oh, wow…… My friend works in the Weapons department. Nice to have you around - perhaps we will work together someday."

"I'll be looking forward to that, sir."

"Now come on, let's get this thing installed..."

The lab has similar pieces of equipment like the Barnes' lab. The striking difference is the size of the quantum computer. It is larger and has more complicated twists and turns of cable than that at Barnes' lab - even bigger than that at the NRL.

The optical laser system is lifted from the forklift and carefully placed on a platform between the quantum computer and custom-built confocal instruments. It is to be connected to both terminals.

Chief directs the installation. Cables from the system are manipulated and linked with a part of the confocal systems.

"Come on, Garret," George urges him.

Garret flicks a hard glance at him and goes forth to help with the installation. As the other two engineers try to link the system with the quantum computer, Garret tries to link it on his side of the system. He knows George asked him to do that as a kind of test and show-off. But he's up for it.

After several manipulations and linking adjustment, the installation is complete. The systems are all powered on. They work just fine. The optical laser system is checked properly by the Chief. It is wholly functional.

Chief runs several diagnostic tests….And now he has that smile of satisfaction on his face.

"Awesome… Finally, our laser system works, thanks to Barnes' Laboratory," Chief comments. "I'll communicate with your boss later."

"All right, Chief. We have to go now," George intones.

"Yeah." He turns to Garret. "Hope to see you again."

"And I you, sir," Garret replies.

One more look at the man at the end of the hall, he follows George toward the truck.

"You know you shouldn't be telling people that I'm from the NRL. Don't wanna say it's embarrassing, but I feel kinda off when they're all on me - you know, asking questions and all."

"Oh... my apologies, man - thought you were cool with it."

"Nah... was just trying to be..."

"Hey!"

That's a call from behind. Both men look back. The cheer in Garret's face vanishes at once at the sight of the man coming toward them. Now it's time - time to ask him who he is and why he's been glaring at him.

"Hello," he greets Garret and nods at George, swishing his finger across his nose. "Can I talk to you for a minute?"

He pulls lightly on his blue suit. Garret looks at George as if to ask for permission. George gives him a nod. He turns back at the man who gestures him to a corner.

"Who the hell are you, and why do I feel like you're stalking me?" Garret huffs.

"Words man, words!" he smiles softly. "If I was gonna keep 'stalking' (making the quotation sign) you, I wouldn't be revealing myself to you... Well, my name is Ziko Kaycee, but you can simply call me Ziko..."

"Okay...?"

"I know what you're looking for, and I can link you up with the right people."

Garret flicks a glance at George as his face darkens at what Ziko said.

"What are you talking about?" he asks.

"You know what I'm talking about - the laboratory equipment. We got them at affordable prices."

He dips his hand into his suit and takes out his business card.

"Here's my card. Call me if you really want the equipment."

Garret is reluctant. He is in a state of limbo at the moment.

"Take it now that your friend isn't looking," Ziko chivvies him.

Garret looks in George's direction, and then back at Ziko. He takes the card, looks at it for a moment and shoves it straight into his pocket - he's not sure he got any information on the card.

"I'll be expecting your call. Have a nice day."

Ziko pulls lightly on his suit and walks away. Garret remains on the spot, watching him as he goes. The thoughts crisscrossing his mind are broken by George's voice.

"Who is he? What does he want?"

Garret snaps out of his confusion and exhales.

"He just wanted to be friends."

"Friends? I don't understand..."

"Keep telling people that I am from the NRL and you will make me a large circle of friends."

Garret smiles half-heartedly and walks toward the truck.

"Oh come on - thought we got past that already."

"Well the man didn't..."

Garret has a myriad of thoughts going on in his head - the most concerning of which is how Ziko found out about his need for the pieces of equipment. They had already seen each other eye to eye before he got on the internet to search for potential marketers. So he could not have learnt about it from there. Could he be keeping tabs on him? Could someone be watching him? Is his townhouse bugged? And even if he decides to give Ziko a call, he doesn't trust him. But seeing him with Chief means he might actually have a source for the pieces of equipment he needs.

Since the truck is yet to leave the J & J Lab, Garret takes the advantage at once.

"Hang on a minute, George."

"Where are you going?"

"I'll be back shortly."

"Don't take too long in there..."

Garret doesn't intend to. He just wants to confirm who Ziko is from Chief.

"Can I talk to you for a minute, sir?" Garret says, standing a few feet away from the door.

"I'll be with you in a minute, son," Chief replies - he is standing behind a colleague while analyzing the data on a computer screen.

He soon joins, Garret, adjusting his coat.

"What is it, son?" he inquires.

"Um, if you don't mind, Chief, could you please tell me who that man with you a moment ago is - the man on blue suit?"

"Why do you ask?"

"He walked up to me and said he could link me up with lab equipment. I'm not sure, but is he with J and J Labs?"

"Nah... Ziko is a broker. He has access to some unique lab equipment. I don't know where he finds it, but he has acquired some rare equipment for us. He knows everyone in the scientific community."

"But..."

"I'm sorry, son - but I have to get back to work. My regards to Barnes."

Chief turns away and walks back to the computer monitor.

Garret may not have gotten all that he wanted, but this bit of confirmation clears some questions in his mind.

He returns to the truck. George has a lot of questions coming as they head back to the lab, but Garret keeps him afloat.

***

At the end of the day's work, Garret is set to leave. However, his confusion leads him to sharing what Ziko told him with Barnes. They are standing outside the building, next to a robot cart.

"There are some marketers in the used and black market who sell the things you want at affordable prices," Barny reveals. "That's true! But I don't patronize them..."

"Why?" Garret asks.

"I don't know - I just don't like them. I'm not saying their products are bad, don't get me wrong. After all, J & J patronizes them. I just prefer getting my equipment from sources I feel are more legit. It's psychological."

Garret sighs. Barny can see the confusion yet willingness to try them out in his face.

"I understand that you want to set up your equipment and get back to your experiment as soon as possible, but I strongly advice you take precautions. Some of these guys in the used market are rippers. Just take your time and study them before you put your money in."

Garret exhales sharply.

"Okay. Thanks Barny. I have to go now," he intones.

"Yeah. I'll see you tomorrow...

CHAPTER FOUR:
INTRODUCTIONS

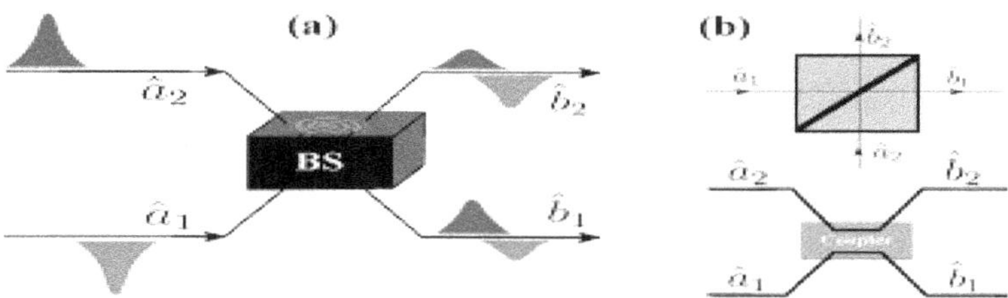

"I received a call from Logan's Photonics last night," Barny informs Garret.

They are sitting at the table in Barny's office. Last night, at 1am, Barny called Garret on the phone, exigently requesting his early presence at his office at dawn. Garret did not stop wondering why he sounded so urgent.

"Their FX Laser 212 Optimizer went down and they want us to come to their lab and fix it…"

"FX Laser Optimizer 212?"

"Yes."

"Whoa, that's huge!"

"It is. And that is why I want you to lead the operation, you have experience with it while you were at the NRL – George will assist you."

"Isn't that, you know…"

"I know, but even he respects what you can do – so you don't have to worry about him. Now I want you to understand that Logan's Photonics is a mega laboratory. They have powerful pieces of equipment that you need for your experiments. Who knows, they might link you up with their dealers, or even grant you access to theirs. So I need you to put in your very best in this."

"I sure will. Thank you for having so much trust in me."

"Then don't blow it. You should be on your way in 20 minutes…"

Garret is still contemplating about contacting Ziko. He was kept awake the whole night with thoughts. His skepticism now stems on the fact that Barny does not patronize the black or used market. And to talk about J & J Lab, he's already discouraged, considering the low-grade laser system they bought probably from the same used market. But on the other hand, he doesn't have enough money to buy new equipment – not even his insurance can cover that. This is one reason the thoughts of trying out the used market are still in his mind.

Garret and George soon arrives at Logan's Photonics. The building is almost the same size with the NRL. The name is printed like a beam of laser inscription on the side of the building

"Please don't tell anyone here that I am from the NRL," Garret tells George as they make it through the opaque glass door.

The door is so gigantic Garret had to turn and look at it again after he spoke to George.

"I'll do my best not to," George teases him, with a smile on his face.

The pieces of equipment here are as sophisticated and powerful as those in the NRL according to Garret's assessment and judgment – some of them here are even more powerful, like the CMOS vacuum accelerator, photon counter and the atomic sequencer. Garret can already guess what it will be like finishing his experiment here.

"Hello, gentlemen. I believe you're from Barnes' Laboratory?" a man in a black suit intones, having intercepted them on their way through the front door of the lab.

"Yes, thank you," Garret says and shakes hands with him.

"Great. I am Maxwell, the Chief Scientist. I don't have to go into detail about what happened to our Laser Optimiser, but we have urgent need for it and are hoping that you can fix it."

"We'll do our best, sir," Garret assures.

"All right. This way, please." Maxwell gestures to a narrow walkway by the left.

He leads the men through. Garret spots the different cooling equipment – so functionally powerful they can cool atoms to a temperature like that in space. If only he could have access to these, he will understand the interaction between the laser beam and the glass molecule, and maybe gain insight on whether the molecules are being teleported to another space or not. This equipment could provide the missing link to Garret's formula.

"This is it."

Maxwell gestures to the FX Laser Optimizer 212. It is nearly the size of a semi-truck. There are cylindrical plates arranged in concentric circles at the center – each plate is about 2cm wider than the one before it. The tip of the circles is like the tiny aperture in a pinhole camera. It is called the pointer. There are buttons and knobs at the top. From the back runs huge turns of cable wires – they are connected to a large terminal on the wall. The Laser itself is placed on a tempered glass plinth. George cocks a brow at the sight of it.

"We're not sure what happened to it, but it just stopped working while we were in the middle of an experiment last night," Maxwell adds.

"Did you check the cables to make sure none of them snapped or is out of place or have overheated?" George inquires.

"Yes, we did, but we found nothing."

Garret is already checking out the Optimizer. He already suspects something. He knows that the equipment has the beam expander, laser control and even the micropositioner built into it. He looks closely at the plates and spots it. With a deep sigh, he turns at Maxwell.

"I think there's a fault in the positioning of the plates," he says.

Maxwell gets closer and adjusts his glasses.

"If you look carefully, you will see that the plates are intricately graduated in micrometers. For the laser to come through the pointer, the plates must all be aligned as one unit. If for any reason any of them is shifted out of place – even as small as 1 micrometer, the laser will be blocked off. It will not come through the pointer. This shift in one plate consequently causes a shift in the others. So to get the laser through the pointer again, we have to reset the whole plate…"

"Okay. How do you do that?" Maxwell asks.

"It is to be done both electronically and manually. First, we will contact the manufacturer with the request for the equipment's skeletal model and coding, using the model number. With the skeletal model, we will reset the plates on the computer backed by the coding system. And when we're done, we will then reset the plates manually, using the template we created on the computer."

"May I ask how long this is going to take?"

"5 hours, maybe more, depending on how fast the manufacturer responds to our request."

"All right. Let's not waste any more time. Go ahead, please. I am sure you know how to get the equipment's model number?"

"Of course," George replies.

"Okay then. Please do not hesitate to reach out to any one of us here if you need anything."

"We won't, sir."

"And you can work with any of those computers over there. Passwords have been input for today's operation," Maxwell points at a set of computers on a table at a corner of the lab.

Garret gets to work. He crouches beside the Optimizer to copy out the model number inscribed on the body. If he can prove himself to Maxwell, he could be allowed to use the lab's pieces of equipment. He could be on a journey to rediscovering his prowess as a scientist – for since he was dismissed from the Navy, even with the fire burning in him to continue his experiment, there is still that voice – that voice that keeps chipping in negative thoughts. But so as not to be too expectant, if nothing comes out of this, there is a partial resolve to contact Ziko.

3hrs later…

Garret and George have been able to get the skeletal model of the Laser Optimizer from the manufacturer and have completed the setup on the computer. Now they work with the template to reset the plates – even the manufacturer provided some assistance as to how to loosen the plates so they will be easy to reset. Maxwell and some other top scientists in the lab have checked in on them, hopeful that their work comes out successful.

Garret carefully rotates the plates one by one according to what George reads from the templates on the computer.

"Wait, how are we supposed to know that they're all properly aligned?" George asks.

"We will hear a sharp click – like a set of springs snapping together."

"Do you have to reset the whole plate before we hear the click?"

"No. It can happen in any one of them – that's actually if I am doing it right, you know…"

"Stop joking around."

"I'm not…"

Now George can't wait to hear that click. He listens carefully even as he directs Garret's hands. He seriously hopes he's doing it right. There's tiredness in his bones and muscles – that's likely because they've only sat down while they were waiting for the manufacturer to respond.

About 7 plates, Garret continues to rotate them. He's in the 5th plate already and yet no click.

"Go 0.2, back 0.1, forward again, 0.2…"

George continues to direct Garret.

4 hours 45 minutes later…

George's hope of them leaving here anytime soon is rapidly evaporating at this time. They spent so much time on the 5th plate. They may be on the 6th plate now, but his knees are wobbling already. Garret himself will not deny the fact that he's tired of screwing back and forth, but he has no choice but to continue.

"Are you sure we're getting out of this today?" George questions.

"I don't know, man. But we have to keep trying…"

"We're on the 6th plate, man. What if…"

"Let's keep trying, George. Focus!"

That's the umpteenth time Garret is bringing George to focus, lest he reads a wrong template to him. George swallows his words and continues.

Not too long, Garret enters the 7th plate. George already concludes they will be on this the whole day.

"0.1 backward – 0.3 forward – 0.2 backward – 0.1 forward…"

George reads on. Garret himself is starting to question why they haven't heard the click yet. He's carefully done all he's supposed to do.

"0.001 backward – 0.002 forward – 0.000 backward… and that is it," George concludes.

Garret turns the 7th plate as he read and stands back. He is sweating across his forehead.

"What went wrong?" he asks himself.

"What do we do now?" George asks, walking closer to him.

Garret does not reply, but gazes at the Optimizer core. Something is definitely missing, he thinks. He goes closer and looks at the graduations on the plates – everything seems aligned.

He goes to the computer and runs a check between the skeletal model and the computer template they designed. He realizes that plate 4 is not properly aligned in the template as in the skeletal model – and that likely affected the graduations. He sets the numbers at the most possible graduations using the skeletal model.

"Please come over here and call the numbers for plate 4," he tells George.

"Plate 4?"

George's brows furrow as he takes over the system again and begins to call the numbers. Garret rotates the plate slowly and carefully.

"0.2 forward – 0.1 backward – 0.1 backward…"

And as Garret turns the plate to the number, the click breaks the silence. It is like a camera's shutter sound. George's mouth spread into a wide smile. There's huge relief on his face. Garret himself could not help but take a deep breath. The smile – the look of satisfaction and feeling of accomplishment all engulf him. He stands back and admires the Laser equipment.

"You did it, man. You did it," George remarks, patting Garret's shoulder.

"Nah, we did it," Garret corrects him.

Maxwell and two other scientists arrive at the scene, with questions in their eyes.

"Were you able to fix it?" Maxwell asks.

"I believe so, sir. You can check it out," Garret answers.

He may be all relieved and excited, but he knows the job is not done until it is tested. The thought of this weakens the smile on his face.

One of the scientists stands by the side of the Optimizer. He clicks some buttons and turns one or two knobs. There is slow whirring, which is followed by a high-pitched sound in the equipment. But as the sound dies down a green laser beam is projected against a screen directly opposite the equipment.

Now the relief in Garret's mind and on his face is complete. The smile on George's face gets wider. The scientists themselves are impressed as per the looks on their faces.

"This is amazing, all systems go," Maxwell remarks. "I must let you men know that three different tech-engineers, even our very own, have tried to fix this equipment, but they all failed. This is not in any way to discredit them, but to let you both, especially you (gesturing at Garret) know that you have achieved what we almost thought was impossible. Personally, I am impressed…"

"I am too," one of the other scientists says.

"Me too. This is incredible!" the other chips in.

"Thank you, sir," George replies.

But Maxwell turns to Garret, and asks:

"What is your name, son?"

"Garret Strong."

"Oh yeah, Garret. Mr. Barnes told me about you. I heard about your mishap at the NRL…" He sighs and rolls his eyes dismissively. "Can't believe a genius like you was sent out of the NRL." He exhales sharply and continues: "well boy, on behalf of all the scientists and engineers at Logan's Photonics, are indebted to you. If you ever have a need to use any of our equipment just give me a shot. You can make use of our facility anytime any day. You can either work solo or with other scientists, including those of us here."

"Wow, I'm so excited, sir…"

"If I may add to what the Chief Scientist said," one of the scientists cuts in. "What he means is that we're willing to partner with you. However, there are no choking terms and conditions in this partnership. We can also deliver any piece of equipment to you from our lab to help you with any project you might wish to undertake. You could actually see it as appreciation for your work.

"Whatever it is, I am grateful, sir. Thank you – thank you for this great offer."

"You're welcome. We are all scientist and we need to stick together. The laboratory is open to you anytime…"

It is overwhelming to Garret that he could be partnering with Logan's Photonics – one of the best laboratories in the nation. It is a pathway to all he hopes to achieve in the world of optics and quantum physics.

However, he still needs to set up his own lab. For his original experiment, he can work on it anywhere. But for the one he discovered accidentally, it has to be done in secret. And that is the reason he needs to set up his own lab. But that does not beat the limitless exploration he will enjoy in this lab.

"Congratulations, man," George says as they make their journey back to their lab.

***

No risk, no reward! Garret thinks it is time he took that risk. He got back from work at 5pm. There was only one thought in his mind: to contact Ziko. And so when he got back from work, he picked up his phone, and called his number.

"Meet me up at the Glade 8pm. I will have to introduce you to some of my contacts. Call me when you get there," Ziko told him.

At 7:30pm, Garret is on his way to the Glades. He has managed to narrow his thoughts to only to options: either he buys from the marketers on the used market or from the black market or he could continue the accidental experiment at Barnes' lab and the original at Logan's Photonics. But he hopes the equipment brokers give him what he wants – he hopes Ziko is not trying to swindle him.

The taxi pulls over by the road. On the left is a narrow sloping bridge– a stream of water flows below it. Beyond the bridge are steel bars in form of barricades. There are people moving about behind the bars. There are also houses built with steel rods. It is like a world on its own.

Garret makes his way through the bridge. The water below is fast-flowing – anything that drops into it is swept away. At this point, Garret's phone is very important, and so he grips it firmly as he crosses.

It is easy to spot a newcomer in this gathering of people. Their bodies are covered with tattoos. Most of them have facial tattoos. Shaved heads or Mohawk's are common with the men – and to the women, scanty dresses. Garret looks quite different. No tattoo's and clean shaven with a full head of hair. With his white shirt and black trouser make a sharp contrast to the faded shirts and torn pants around him. And from the way Garret looks, the people can easily tell he's not one of them – most of them have their eyes on him as he walks past.

Now he is fully inside the Glades. There are ramshackle buildings everywhere. These buildings are built right above water. Because the water covers most parts of the Glade, there are boats to get to one building and another. Steel pilings hold up the buildings which are right above the waterline.

But even with the seemingly cheap standard of living here, life still goes on a normal course. The Glade is always busy. The men and the women smoke like chimneys and drink like fishes. You can buy any drug you desire. The ladies leave their breasts barely covered – an attraction for potential clients.

Prostitution is the number business next to drug dealing. As Garret walks deeper into the Glade the riff-raft seems to get worse.

And finally, he settles on a spot behind a pole – a spot he found safe enough to take out his phone. He puts a call across to Ziko's line.

"Where are you?" Ziko asks.

"Uh... I don't know, but there's a building here – there's something written on it..."

"What is it?"

"It's not clear enough, but I think it's Scr–Screw Dogs."

"Okay. Stay there, I'll be with you soon..."

Garret hangs up, and continues to feed his eyes.

"How do these people survive?" he questions in his mind.

There are lots of questions to ask about this place – but he knows he's not getting the answers any time soon – best to enjoy the view while it lasts.

"Hello handsome," a lady cruises by.

Her shirt is unbuttoned and her breasts are on full display, dangling freely across her chest. Garret looks at her in the face, and spares a moment on her breasts.

"You like what you see?" she asks.

"Yeah, but I think I'll pass," he replies.

"Loser!"

She storms away, onto the next victim. Garret glances at her tattooed backside and returns his attention to his phone. He slides his thumb on it. He wants to call Ziko again, but his voice comes from behind.

"You don't have to do that."

Garret turns sharply. Ziko is dressed casually this time – not in his blue suit like the last time, and that consequently reveals his slim frame. He's got neck-chain that glints in the orange lights of the Glade.

"Come with me," he tells Garret.

They walk along a narrow path. Garret has his eyes everywhere. He still doesn't trust Ziko. This could all be a setup he designed to cash out from.

"What is the place?" Garret finally lets out the question he's been carrying in his mind since he got here.

"It's a jungle, with a government of its own," Ziko answers. "There's freedom here – no suffocation from the stupid laws made by the government. Whatever you need is here – money, love, sex, drugs and power – you can still get the opposite of all of that –depends on your mindset."

Garret swallows back the rest of the question. He should be more interested in what he is here for, he thinks.

Ziko's movements soon decelerate. He and Garret are standing at the waterside. There's a small steel bridge that leads through some distance to a houseboat.

"I'm taking you to some men – men who can give you all that you want – equipment, software – just anything," Ziko says. "I hope you have good bargaining power, 'cause that's what's gonna save you in there?"

He continues walking – Garret follows. He thought they were going into the houseboat.

"I have to see the equipment first before bargaining, right?" he asks.

"I don't know – depends on them. They can decide to send you pictures…"

"Pictures? I thought it was physical?"

"You only see the pieces of equipment physically after you've confirmed the deal. No shady deals, you pay upon delivery – and that is the only moment you get to see the things you're buying…"

Now they get to a building high over the water. Ziko mounts a small boat.

"Get in," he urges Garret.

With a bit of hesitation, Garret mounts the boat too. Ziko directs the boat to a steel staircase hanging down into the water.

He disembarks and gets on the staircase – Garret quickly follows. Their footsteps thud against the staircase as they ascend.

They soon arrive at a passageway. Ziko leads the way. It's a den of debauchery – smoking, drinking and having sex. Garret glances into the rooms as he walks by.

"There is no time, so you have to make it quick. You understand everything I told you?" Ziko intones, standing next to the door of a room.

"Yeah," Garret replies.

Ziko turns and walks into the room. Garret does not follow immediately this time, but stands by the door.

"Come on in, man," Ziko calls.

Garret walks in to behold three men thought to be in their 50s. There are all in suits. The looks on their faces are not inviting at all. But it appears they have been waiting far too long. One of them is rather large. He's about three times Garret's size – and five times Ziko's size.

"I'm sorry for keeping you guys waiting," Ziko apologizes. "This is the man I told you about – my man, Garret. He's a brother, so be fair with your prices."

He turns to Garret.

"Hey man, this (pointing at the first man) is Vladimir from Russia, this (second) is Lu Chang from China, and this (third – the large man) is Yang from Japan. I'm sure you know these are countries you will find the best of equipment. Come on, have a seat."

"Hi," Garret greets.

He moves closer and shakes hands with the men and then settles himself on the only chair remaining in the untidy room that reeks of alcohol.

"So, let's get straight to business: what do you want?" Yang intones in the Japanese accent, adjusting his bottom on the easy chair.

Garret clears his throat.

"I need good scientific equipment for my laboratory."

Vladimir sighs.

"Well, this meeting is basically for every one of us here to know that we are not working with ghosts," Vladimir speaks in the typical Russian accent. "The time of bargaining prices at first meeting is over (Garret glances at Ziko on hearing that). So we will give you our email. You will officially prepare an order and send it to us. We will send you the prices of every order you made. You can either start a bargain via email, or you schedule an appointment with us. We will always be present. That is something unique about the business: it is flexible and transparent. You can trust us."

"You will have to be very specific of the particular equipment you want, very specific with model numbers and power output." Yang adds in the Japanese accent. "It is very important, so we don't give you the price of another piece or even bring it here and waste all of our time."

"And please, keep our conversation with you private. There must be no fourth party," Lu Chang warns.

Garret flicks a glance at Ziko and turns to the men.

"I believe payment is made on delivery?"

"Exactly!" Lu Chang affirms.

"And how long does it take to deliver after an agreement has been established?"

"5 to 10 working days."

Garret exhales. He stays quiet for a moment. The men know he's making a decision in his mind, so they wait patiently. Ziko too is patient, although he seems sure Garret will accept the deal.

"Okay," Garret breaks the silence. "I'll go ahead and give you my list of lab equipment. So how do I get your email address?"

"You will receive it from Ziko, he is your broker," Vladimir says.

"All right then."

Garret gets on his feet.

"It was nice meeting you guys," he says, stretching forth his hand.

The men give him a handshake one after the other. And then he turns to Ziko.

"I gotta go," he says, walking out the door.

Ziko follows him.

Now they stand in the passageway, talking.

"What do you think?" Ziko inquires.

"It's interesting. I will send them an email. I need the equipment as soon as possible, so I wouldn't want to be the cause of the delay. But I do hope the prices are affordable like you made me believe."

"You still have to bargain with them – that's the flexibility."

"I sure will. I have to go now."

"All right. You know your way out?"

"Sure!"

"Okay. Talk to you later."

Garret makes his way down the stairs.

"Hey!" Ziko calls.

Garret turns.

"Make sure you send your list to them today, okay?"

Garret does not reply, but looks at him for a while and then continues on his way down. He now knows why Ziko is so concerned about the deal going successfully. It's because of the financial benefits involved such as his brokers fee. Garret wonders how much commission Ziko gets for the introduction and the sale.

As Garret makes it out of the Glade, he hears a croaky voice from behind.

"Hey you!"

Garret turns around. He thinks it's Ziko. His eyes search the space, but he does not see Ziko anywhere. As he turns to continue on his way, the voice comes again:

"I'm talking to you punk…"

Garret looks in the direction the voice had come. Three hulky men leaning against a wall of graffiti, cigarettes dangling from their mouths. Their eyes meet those of Garret's behind a cloud of smoke.

"Get over here," the man in the middle orders, presumably the leader of the gang. He looks bigger than the other two.

But Garret doesn't seem intimidated by their size. He ignores the call and walks on. That aggravated the men. They storm toward him. With the look of aggravation on their faces, Garret appears to be in serious trouble.

He hears the men's footsteps thumping closer, and quickly turns around. Now he is standing right in front of them. – eyes fixed on their hands.

"Quite clear you're not one of us," the leader observes with a sneer. He and his men quickly cover the exit in case Garret tries to run. "What's your name punk?"

"Who's asking?" Garret replies. He balls his hand into a fist – eyes focused on their next move.

The leader gives a sideway smile and looks at his men standing on both sides. The scar across his forehead is probably that of battle – a possible mark of years of thuggery.

"I like your guts. But you see," he takes a step closer to Garret, "in here, we rule. Now let me have your phone and wallet."

Garret's face loses all expression. His muscles are toned for what is about to happen.

"What for?" he questions.

The leader sighs and cracks his knuckles as a way of intimidation. But maybe if he observed closely, he would notice that neither his looks nor his actions instilled fear in Garret. Years of training developed Garret to be ready for anything. It didn't matter if Garrets enemy was stronger, faster or bigger he was trained to handle anything.

"You don't know who we are – and that is why I am being gentle with you. But it's starting to evaporate, and I can't hold back any longer. Give me your phone and everything you have in your pockets."

"No, I don't think I'm going to do that. Now, please get out of my way."

The leader smiles and glances at his men once again. He turns back to Garret and nods.

"All right," he agrees, raising his hands and stepping aside.

Garret doesn't have to be told that that's a ploy to attack him. He is still fully at alert. And as he takes a step forward, the leader sends a heavy punch toward his face. Garret catches the thug's hand and delivers a punch to the man's shoulder weakening his arm. The leader falls backward in astonishment.

The other two men charge in. One of them flings a blow from the back – Garret bends and glides behind him, firing a punch to the back of his head. The third man moves in quickly and grabs Garret by the waist. It is for a chance for the other two to hurt him. But Garret almost breaks his spine with a double elbow to his collar bone snapping it like a chicken bone. He lets out a loud cry of pain. As he falls backward, still bent at the waist, Garret gives him a knee to the face. He crashes to the ground moaning in pain.

"You bastard!" the leader growls.

As he charges closer, Garret takes a leap and fires a direct kick to his head. He staggers and falls. The other man grabs Garret by the waist. But his grip is weak. Garret easily fights free and grabs his waist from behind. He lifts him up and slams him on the hard ground compressing his head like a pancake on the cement.

Garret pulls up the leader, throttling him by the collar of his shirt.

"You ask questions first before you try to mess around with someone," he huffs.

Despite the man's size, Garret lifts him off the ground and hurls him into the water behind. His weight sends a huge splash of water.

With the three men knocked down, Garret is the last man standing. He observes that they are down and then turns to continue on his way. Running down the sidewalk towards Garret a fourth man picks up a steel pipe that he found on the ground. Unfortunately, he does not use it. Garret is fast enough to disarm him as he tries to smash his head with it. With an upper cut Garret smites his jaw with the pipe. The impact is so loud his jaw must have broken into pieces. He grunts in pain and then falls into the gutter, giving way for Garret to leave.

Garret may have won the fight now, but he will have more men to deal with the next time he comes to the Glade. Ziko might not be able to save him when that time comes. He will have to fight his way out again. Its best that Garret never returns to the Glade.

CHAPTER FIVE:
HELLO JUDY

$$\phi = 2/\left(\sqrt{5} + 1\right)$$

George and Daniel finish their work on the custom confocal system. They are standing by it and explaining some of the features to Garret.

"Every accessory you need to maintain precise projection and focus is built in," George says. "You got the micropositioners, the cameras – we couldn't get our hands on the CMOS camera, so we used the CCD instead. Right here (gesturing at the middle of the unit) are the laser focusing lenses. They support the work of the microlaserpositioners to bring the image to a perfect focus. You have the laser sensors and the wavelength selective switch amongst others."

"And right here," Daniel gestures, "are high resolution objectives. They give large FOV and long working distance. You also have the laser scanning unit, with a Widefield Fluorescence Illumination Port and good emission beamsplitters…"

Garret looks impressed, walking round the equipment and skimming his fingers across different parts of it.

"Wow, this is truly beyond my expectations," he comments.

"We told you that you were gonna like it," George replies. "So you got all you need to get back to your experiment."

"Thanks guys, I really appreciate it…"

"Hey Garret!" a voice calls from behind.

Garret turns to behold a lady in a lab coat. He is surprised that she knows his name.

"The boss wants to see you," she reports.

"Yo, Judy, welcome back," George hails.

"Thank you…"

Garret turns back to the men.

"I haven't seen her before. Who is she?" he asks.

"A PhD student – lost her brother two weeks ago, and was granted some time off by Mr. Barnes," Daniel answers.

"She's pretty intelligent, MIT graduate. You'll both make a great team."

"Can't be so sure about that," Garret replies. "See you guys later."

He shuffles off to Barny's office. Now he has the custom-built microscope, it is time to fully get back to his experiment. It is time to find out what went wrong the first time. The equipment may not be as sophisticated as the one in the NRL, but it sure has some unique features to it.

"There's a conference tomorrow, organized by the Global Technological Inventors Organization," Barny tells him. "The conference is about the advancements of technology and the challenges faced by inventors. Powerful men and women in the organization will be present at this conference. I want you to accompany me to this conference. You will meet and talk with the elite in the organization. It is a way of exposing you to opportunities. The time is 11am."

"All right. I'll be there. Thank…"

"We're going together in my car," Barny cuts in. "And don't worry – you won't get too bored with me. Judy is also going with us…"

"Yeah, I just saw her. George says she's an intern and very smart…"

"That's correct – she's been gone for two weeks for personal reasons. That's why you didn't see her when you came. She could help you in your experiment – you know, run a couple of errands."

"Nah, I'll be fine…"

"By the way, you still in contact with those marketers?"

Garret scratches his chin, a bit hesitant to answer.

"Did something happen?" Barny asks, having observed the look on his face.

"Not really! Just thinking about ways to get the money complete – it's not easy, you know. We're talking $500,000 here. Five to ten working days – and I've already lost three days."

"Don't let your heart boil up, son – we'll get those pieces of equipment. As much as I don't fancy getting these things from the used market, I having a feeling this is going to turn out right for you. Let me know when it's time for delivery."

"Of course, I will," Garret assures.

As he steps out of Mr. Barnes' office, he bumps in on Judy. The thought of why Barny wants to go with him to the delivery site vanishes at once at the sight of her. Garret will admit she's beautiful. With full blonde hair, aquiline nose and thin pouty lips, even in what seems like an oversized lab coat, she still has the features of a swimsuit model. And all that beauty is garnished with a dimple when she smiles. However, the dark shadows beneath each of her eyes suggests she must have cried a river over her brother's death.

"Hi," Garret greets.

"Hi Garret. You must be wondering how I got to know your name even before we met." Judy intones casually.

"Yeah. But seeing you come from the boss's office, I knew he must have told you my name…"

"Not just your name – a lot more."

"Whoa! A lot more like?"

"Being your chemistry teacher in high school, and you being an enthusiastic physicist – I don't think there was any exaggeration – not much."

"That's me…"

"Well…"

"I was told you're a PhD student and acquired your master from MIT."

"Now that's a true definition of 'pretty much'."

Garret giggles.

"Well…"

"All right, Garret – nice to meet you. I've got to go now."

"Nice to meet you too…"

Judy walks off to the Nanofabricating Prototyping Clean Room of the lab.

"Pretty jovial," Garret comments.

Judy can actually make a good workmate, he thinks. He can try to bring her into his original project. The teleportation project, he must work on alone. It's a top-secret project, although it is his aim to expand Mr. Barnes' lab with the incoming lab equipment.

***

Garret is still in the lab at 9pm. He has resumed the experiment to understand the interaction of light and opaque body.

In the first experiment, the computer revealed multiple streaks of light when the laser hit the bio sample. His aim at that time was to find a way to produce a single streak on the computer. And so he had to increase the frequency and wavelength of the laser light, which ultimately led to the destructions in the lab.

This time, he has another possible explanation as to why he got multiple streaks and a laser tornado:

"Maybe I have to cool the atoms of the molecule way below absolute zero temperature," he thinks.

It is clear to him that he may not have cooled the atoms of the bio sample enough to slow them down - for if they were slow enough, a laser bombardment would have been easy - maybe he would have gotten a single streak on the system.

He walks off to the Nanofabricating Prototyping Clean Room to collect the bio sample.

He does not expect to find anyone in the lab at this time, but there she is - Judy. She is still dressed in her lab coat and surgical gloves working on an experiment.

"You're still here?" Garret asks.

"Yes. Having been away from work for two weeks, I have to get some samples ready for collections. We're not the only ones that need them, you know - some other labs do."

"Oh..."

63

"What about you: what are you still doing here?"

"I'm working something out."

"Uh... do you mind telling me what it is?"

"You see, not much have been said about what happens when light meets an opaque body, especially a bio opaque body. I have a feeling that when this is understood fully, it could come in handy in criminology. The X-ray lithography technique will be employed here to understand this interaction better. That is what I am working on."

"That's brilliant. Not only in criminology – it could also be employed in cancer therapy and radiography. It could help reduce the complications and risks involved in such therapies and might even provide less invasive treatments."

"Exactly what I'm thinking too. But right now, I'm in the preliminary stage..."

"And I guess you're here to collect a sample?"

"Yes."

"What type?"

"A sample – a single molecule of a piece of bone."

"Okay. Please check those cabinets over there," Judy points at a glass case on her right.

Garret goes for it. Judy is indeed as brilliant as they say she is, he thinks. How quick she is to relate other fields his experiment could prove really useful is impressive to him. But he knows Barny always has a thing for the best and the smartest.

With the sample safely collected in a small glass, he heads out.

"See you later, Judy..."

"Um... Garret," she calls.

Garret turns.

"Do you mind if I join you in your experiment? We can work together, you know. I may not have the experience that you have, but I feel that I can also contribute a little to it, and I will learn a lot too."

Garret takes a moment of reluctance. He wanted this to be a solo experiment, now it seems like he has no choice but to accept a second hand.

"Sure. You can join me..."

"Yay! Thank you. I'll be there as soon as I'm done here. But it's not just for tonight, right?"

"No, anytime."

Judy does not notice that his acceptance appears forced, very forced.

"Okay. Thanks," she replies.

"No problem..."

Garret turns his face awkwardly and walks away. The fact that Judy remains in the lab even at night makes him uncomfortable. He will find a way to keep the teleportation project as hidden as possible.

Garret returns to his department and places the bio sample in an X-Series Laser Cooling system. This equipment works with the principle of atomic spectroscopy and the mechanical effect of light to compress the velocity of the atoms, thereby cooling it in a photon absorption- emission fashion. The whole process takes less than a minute.

Now Garret stands and watches as the equipment does its work. He tries to keep his mind focused so as not to make any mistake this time, even though it tends to wander off to how he will complete the money for the purchase.

He has just projected the sample to the confocal system and is headed toward it when Judy walks in.

"Hey, what are you up to?" She has her hand in her pockets and a smile on her face.

"Nothing much... I have just cooled the sample and projected it to the core. Now it's time for bombardment..."

Garret put on his eye tracker and watches the core carefully.

"Let's see," he hears Judy say.

She too picks up an eye tracker on a table nearby and puts it on. She goes and stands next to Garret.

"You can see the laser traveling through the micropositioners to reach the sample," he explains.

"Yes, I can see that. The results are expected to be collected on the screen, right?"

"Yes..."

Garret removes the eye tracker and goes to the objective lens. He looks through to know if the sample is being bombarded at the right position.

After a while, he projects the results on the screen to the computer. It seems like he has finally beat this particular step. He hurries to the chair, and starts to input data into the computer.

The analysis by the computer is the same. The multiple streaks are shown, and are seemingly much brighter this time. The look of disappointment is once again crested on Garret's face. He stares at the result in front of him.

"You don't look too happy. Is something wrong?" Judy observes.

"The streaks! I'm supposed to get a single streak of light, not multiple circular streaks. Using a single molecule and a single beam, I thought I would get a single streak. Something is not right, and I can't quite place what it is. Perhaps my formula is missing a small element – I don't know."

Judy keeps a thoughtful silence for a moment. She looks carefully at the computer screen, and then at the photon counter in the confocal system.

"Wait, maybe you should read the details on the photon counter," she suggests. "These multiple streaks of light could be as a result of the emission of multiple photons from the atom."

"I have done that again and again. There is emission of multiple photons from the sample. The surprising fact is that the sample absorbs a single photon of light – how then do they emit multiple photons…"

"Then maybe your analysis should be on the sample – or maybe you should work with the multiple streaks."

"I can't. I just have to find a way to produce a single streak. But like you said, maybe I have to change the formula or rethink my analysis approach … maybe I should try bending the laser beam and not try to change the circular light transfer …"

"Bending a laser beam?" Judy's brows snap.

"Yeah, I know it's weird how it naturally wants to bend and twist. It's just not part of any formula or theory…"

***

Garret continued to work on his experiment until 3am. He is faced with the same problem no matter how many times he tried, or which method he employed. He tried to not get frustrated. Judy stayed up with him – although at the time, she was feeling sleepy. He too thought it was best he left it for a while and get some sleep.

However, at 5am, he was thrown awake by Barny's call. It was to remind Garret about the conference later in the day. After the call, Garret straggled up and went home to get ready for the conference, and maybe get some more sleep too before the time.

And now, the three guests pull up at the conference in Mr. Barnes' Tesla. All dressed for the occasion, Mr. Barnes is wearing a black suit and a white shirt beneath it. He's had his hair nicely treated. Now he looks like how the name 'Barny' makes him feel – young. Garret is also wearing a suit. His broad shoulder and well-crafted body in the military fashion sit well in the suit. His hair has been blown and styled. Of course, his face wears a bright glow – not a hint that he has not had enough sleep since last night. Even Judy gulped down a lump of saliva at the sight of him.

"You look good," she complimented.

"Thank you. You don't look bad either," Garret replied.

And with those piercing hazel eyes of his, he is preceded by the charisma of a scientist. Judy herself is wearing a black gown. Her blondeness is not regular. Her hair glows with a mixture of brown and golden – and having been placed in rollers, it falls down her back like water down a ridged hill. Her pouty peach-colored lips are a thing to fancy. Her downturned eyes can keep a man enthralled in her presence – luckily, Garret has not fallen into that temptation yet.

It is 11am and the conference is about to start. Other guests are still arriving. Mr. Barnes leads Garret and Judy into the hall. It is a large space, with pews arranged in rows for the guests. Behind the podium is a large screen showing the growth of technology from the early days till most recently in quick succession. Mr. Barnes and his workers settle in a row somewhere in the middle of the hall.

Shortly after, a man ascends the stairs to the podium. The display on the screen is paused, and the hall regains quiescence.

"Good morning, ladies and gentlemen. You are welcome to the 35th meeting of the scientific technological society. The aim of this conference is to discuss the advancements of technology and the diverse challenges faced by science in the modern world. We will also witness demonstrations by the representatives of two different companies. On that note, I hereby invite Dr. Katherine Gomez to the podium. Dr. Katherine, please…"

A round of applause is raised as a woman in her 50s makes her way to the podium, with papers in her hand. Her full black hair bounces abundantly on her back as she walks.

"I hope to be like her someday," Judy whispers to Garret.

"That's a lot of hard work through years. But of course, you can be like her – maybe even better…"

Mr. Barnes flicks a glance at them – that breaks the whispering.

"Thank you, Dr. Lance. I must say that I am most honored to be here in front of all of you great intellects. The advancement of science and technology over the years cannot be overemphasized. We have all witnessed groundbreaking inventions in the five major categories of technology – the medical, the mechanical, the electronic, the manufacturing, and communication. We can say that the most common of these is perhaps in the electronic technology – the cell phone. But whether common or not, every single one of them have in one way or another improved our lives. Today, we cannot do without them. And scientists all across the world continue to work day and night to discover new technologies, stretching the boundaries even farther. However…"

Mr. Barnes turns to Garret.

"That man on white suit over there (gesturing with his head) – you see him?"

Garret follows the direction of his head and spots the man in the white suit. He is bald and tall, with a handlebar mustache. He is sitting two rows to the right.

"Yes, I see him. Who is he?"

"He is the CEO of Allied Corporations – the largest manufacturer of laboratory facilities in the country, with a market value of more than a billion dollars. He has a thing for bright brains like yours. You can try and have a word with him later on. You could get lucky…"

"You really want me to talk to him, Barny?" Garret asks, with a light fold between his brows.

"Yes, why?"

Garret recoils against the chair – his mind thoughtful. He leaves Barny's question unanswered for a while, before speaking again.

"Why are you pushing me towards these top companies? I mean, why are you linking me up with them? What if they offer me a job – would you like that I take it? I mean, don't you like that I'm working for you?"

Too many questions for Barny. He wonders for how long Garret has been thinking about them – what could be going on in his mind.

"Listen son, like I told you before, I am exposing you to opportunities. You're still very young and have great potential. Mine is a small laboratory. And yes, I like that you are working for or rather, with me. But with me, I don't think you can reach your potential. So I am sending you out to the people I believe will set you up on a higher pedestal than Barnes' Laboratory. There's a lot more to explore in quantum light physics. If they offer you a job in their company or laboratory, I will personally kick you out of my lab to go grab it. So do as I say and stop asking silly questions."

Garret already knows what his answer will be. It is true that his laboratory is quite small and cannot give him all that he wants, but there is room for expansion. And that is what he intends to do when his equipment arrives. Barny on the other hand, has no thought of that. In fact, he wants Garret to establish his laboratory and not to work under him or possibly no one else – that way, his exploits will not be restricted.

The hall has become a bit rowdy. The inaugural lecture is over. There is indistinct chattering amongst the crowd as they all try to mingle. Mr. Barnes is talking with a group of men somewhere in the hall – far away from where they were sitting.

"Mingle, socialize." These were the words he said to Garret before leaving his seat with Judy.

Garret has his eyes on the CEO who is talking with a group of men and women at the moment. He is waiting for when he will be alone so he can move in. But perhaps now is the time – the men and women around the CEO can be of greater help to him than the CEO himself. He does not see it that way, nonetheless. By the way, he does not even know what to do or say to get the CEO's attention.

There should be a unique way to get the attention of a man of his status, instead of the boring meet-and-greet with small talk ensuing, he thinks. But what way is it?

While Garret considers his best means of approach, he notices the CEO walking toward another group of men. It's time!

He gets off the chair, adjusts his suit and makes the pursuit. The CEO is closing in on the men. Garret walks faster.

"Hello sir," he greets from a few feet away.

Luckily, the CEO turns. His handle-bar mustache appears to flare a bit at the sight of Garret as though he has seen him before. The look on his face is enough to make Garret change his mind about talking with him. But he is here already – no going back.

Garret finally gets to where he is.

"You look familiar, son. Have we met before?" the CEO asks, surprisingly in a casual tone of voice.

"Uh… I don't remember meeting you before, sir. I'm sorry," Garret replies as politely as he can.

The CEO bats his eyebrow. He doesn't seem convinced.

"What is your name, son?"

"Garret Strong."

"Garret! That's it! (Now he has a smile on his face) Do you think your brilliance both in high school and in the Navy will go unnoticed?"

Garret is still lost as to where they met. He manages to force what he thinks is a humble smile across on his face.

"The Allied Corporations sometimes take a tour to different schools, looking for bright students like you in the sciences. I, personally, was at your school the day you were crowned as an honor student. I was also there when you were dubbed 'outstanding' by your principal officers. My company is a major supplier of lab equipment to the Navy. So we have a good relationship with them. I was looking forward to talking with you after you were fully inducted as a Naval Officer and were still obtaining your master's degree, but I didn't get the chance to do that. I was later told that you were dismissed from the Navy on account of protocol breach. Now, looking at you, I see a man standing before me."

"I am honored, sir."

Garret has a smile on his face. But in his mind, he is not sure where this conversation will lead, seeing that the man knows about the accident in the NRL. There's already a kind of lethargy in him.

"Come on – let's have a seat," he gestures at a row of chairs next to them.

Garret follows, trying as much as he can to keep a cheerful disposition. But maybe he hasn't noticed that the CEO wanting to talk more with him means he doesn't care about what happened in the lab.

"I guess you were working on a project when the accident happened in the lab?" the CEO presses further.

"Yes sir. It was completely unexpected. But maybe I deserve the punishment in as much as I think it was pretty harsh."

"No, you didn't deserve the punishment. It was too harsh. A different punishment could have been handed out – I told them that. You're a scientist, and accidents like that are expected in every laboratory. You don't get it right all the time. That's why there's insurance to cover for such damages."

"Thank you for speaking up for me, sir."

"Nah, you're a scientist like me, so I understand how these things work. But tell me, what project were you working on?"

Garret only had a split second to decide on which of the projects to tell him – but it isn't enough.

"I was working on the interaction between light and opaque bodies," he blurts. "I feel that there is not enough detail yet as to what happens when light meets an opaque body. I want to understand the principal's involved as to why light cannot travel through an opaque body…"

"But haven't those principles been employed in X-ray?"

"Yes, they have, but this could be more advanced. If successful, it could be less risky in the treatment of cancer than radiation or chemotherapy. It could also be employed in criminology."

"That's pretty interesting!" the CEO remarks. "And how far have you gone with the project?"

"I've not really been working on it since I was thrown out of the Navy. It's more of theoretical than practical. Currently, I work at Barnes' Laboratory for Quantum Physics. I'm still trying to set up the facilities needed for the project. It's not been easy though. But I hope to get back to it fully soon."

The CEO is quiet, thoughtful of what Garret said. At first, Garret was regretful for bringing up the light-and-opaque body project. He thought the teleport project would make more sense to the CEO. But now he is glad he did not make that mistake. The teleport project is supposed to remain a secret no matter who's involved.

"What if you come over to the Allied Laboratories and complete your project? We have all the equipment that you need," the CEO suggests.

"I am most honored, sir – I truly am. But in as much as I would love to complete my project in a well-equipped laboratory like yours, I don't think it is time for me to leave Barnes' Laboratory just yet. I have already established myself there, and I am working on a different project with them. It would not be right if I leave now. I truly hope you understand, sir."

"I understand that you are in a way committed to your current place of work, but the Allied Laboratories will offer you a lot more. There are no limitations to what you can achieve with us."

"I know I will be offered greater exposure in your laboratory. But while I work to get my own facilities, my loyalty is still with Barnes' Laboratory, sir. I'm sorry."

Garret does not mind that he could be blocking off a helping hand from the Allied Corporations – the same company Mr. Barnes urged him to try to get close to. But he just doesn't see himself leaving his best friend's lab anytime soon – that's if he will ever leave.

"I see your mind is made up," the CEO exhales.

"It is, sir."

The CEO sighs and clicks his tongue. Garret is convinced the conversation is over. He now waits for the man to walk away. However…

"Well, for the sake of advancement, which is the reason why we're all here, the Allied Corporation will support your project with some of the equipment you need. This is completely free of charge. You will be provided with software applications necessary for your project. How about that?"

"I am delighted already, sir. It would be great. Thank you so much..."

"It's okay. We will make that available at Barnes' Laboratory in two days. Here…"

He shoves his hand in his suit and takes out his card.

"Call me," he says, handing the card to Garret.

"I definitely will, sir. Thank you…"

CHAPTER SIX: THE EQUIPMENT

$$H(t) \mid \psi(t)\rangle = i\hbar \frac{d}{dt} \mid \psi(t)\rangle$$

The shores of Tiber Creek – that is the rendezvous. It is not too far from the Glade. Garret and Mr. Barnes are on their way there. Ziko and the marketers are already there with the lab equipment.

Garret drives the truck with certain lightness in his hands. There was a miracle – one he did not quite expect. Mr. Barnes contributed his life savings to make up the money. It happened this morning – and Garret is flushed with appreciation ever since.

"I am proud of you, son. I am proud of your efforts. I'm sure your parents are as well. I believe in your potentials, and that is why I am doing this…"

These words came with the money.

"Thank you, Barny," Garret said.

Just three words, yet they meant a lot to him – they carried the abundance of joy in his heart. And obviously, Barny could see it. More words weren't needed.

Tiber Creek is about a kilometer away. Garret thinks it is time to make his intentions known to Barny before they get there.

"With the lab equipment we will expand Barnes' Laboratory. I am not setting up my own laboratory."

Barny turns to him, with an unfamiliar countenance. He doesn't seem to get the message.

"That is what you should do, son – set up your own laboratory. It is what every scientist looks forward to."

"We are expanding Barnes' Laboratory, and you are not talking me out of this one."

"Are you sure about this?"

"Is the pope a catholic?"

Mr. Barnes chuckles. There's no point stressing it.

The truck finally pulls over at the shore of Tibet Creek, in front of Ziko and the other men. Ziko and Vladimir are leaning against a large box truck. The other men are in another van. Garret observes the area to be sure it is not under siege.

"Clear!" Garret says to himself.

They both step out of the car onto the dirty sandy road. Mr. Barnes has all the information ready for a bank transfer.

"Welcome, my friend. Glad you kept to your word," Ziko says, shaking hands with Garret. "Hello," he nods his head at Mr. Barnes.

Lu Chang and Yang get down from the van.

"You have the money?" Vladimir asks.

"I do," Garret answers. Ziko looks down at Mr. Barnes' phone. "All I need is a banking routing number and an account number." Ziko's face registers a light smile. "What about the equipment?"

"In the van," Lu Chang answers.

"We check them out first, right?"

"Right!"

Garret nods at Barny, and they trudge closer to the truck. Ziko and Lu open the doors at the back.

Barny stands outside while Garret goes in and inspects the supplies. He does not take long before coming out.

"How do we know they are in good working conditions?" he asks.

"We are businessmen," Yang replies. "We don't do shady deals. You have 6 months' warranty on each of those pieces of equipment – that's half of that in the official market. If any of them develops a fault within this time, you let us know. We've got great engineers…"

"But we can assure you that they are all in good condition," Lu throws in.

Garret looks at Barny. He shrugs.

"All right. Let's get them loaded into the truck."

The men assisted Garret and Barny in loading the pieces of equipment into the truck – electro-absorption modulated laser, Kinetic plate imager, turnable laser system, even a multimode plate reader, and more.

After they finish loading, Garret turns to Barny to make the transfer. There's reluctance in Barny's hands – not because he feels bad for contributing his life's savings, but because he does not trust the men. It is obvious with the look in his eyes.

"Let me have your account information so I can wire the money," Mr. Barnes requests.

Vladimir gladly provides the details. Garret can almost see the smile hiding in his face. Mr. Barnes taps on his phone. And after a moment, he raises his face.

"Done! Please confirm."

Vladimir takes out his phone from his pocket and logs into his bank account. There's a smile on his face when he looks up. He turns to Yang and Lu Chang and gives a confirmatory nod. Smiles break off their faces.

"It's nice doing business with you, Mr. Garret," Vladimir says.

He shakes hands with him – Yang and Lu Chang too.

"Careful with the equipment – they are fragile," Yang warns. "Let me know if you need anything else."

"Yeah…"

The three men trudge to the vehicles. Ziko walks closer to Garret, with a sly smile on his face.

"You got all you need now…"

"Yeah. Thanks for the help," Garret replies.

"That means we're looking forward to a successful project then?"

Garret's brows crease slightly. That sounds as though Ziko knows why he bought the facilities. But of course not – there's no way he could have known.

"We will meet again," he tells Garret.

That smile remains on his face as he turns back and walks back toward the van. Garret is still on the spot, reading meanings to his words.

"I think you should be more careful with that guy," Barny says he is standing a few feet behind Garret.

"I know. But hopefully this is the only time I'll have to do any kind of business with him. I don't trust him. There's this unusual feeling I get each time I'm around him."

The van in front of them is already driving off the dirty road and heading toward the highway.

"Let's get out of here," Barny tells Garret.

"Yeah, come on…"

And finally, Garret gets almost all the lab equipment he needs to expand Barnes' Laboratory – all the pieces of equipment he needs to take finish the teleportation project. He expects that later in the day, Logan's Photonics will deliver the pieces of equipment they promised him. And tomorrow, he will get more from Allied Corporations. Barny expressed his delight when he told him about the promise by the CEO – although he reprimanded him for not accepting the offer to work with the corporation.

But even as they drive back to the lab, Garret continues to rummage over Ziko's perceived keen interest on his experiment. He is yet to know how he found out that he is dire need of laboratory equipment in the first place. He hopes his business with him does not raise dusts later. However, a feeling continues to linger inside of him – like he is being watched, or even followed – perhaps at the time he and Mr. Barnes were carrying out their lab experiments. And that leaves him cautious of his surroundings.

***

The workers at Barnes' Laboratory, including Garret and Mr. Barnes spent almost the whole day installing the pieces of equipment. Garret was relieved that none of them was faulty. And then the day ended as expected. Logan's Photonics fulfilled their promise and delivered some very sophisticated pieces of equipment to the lab. The installations are to be done the next day together with the equipment and software applications from Allied Corporation.

At 7pm, Judy and Garret are on their way home. He wants to resume his experiments fully after the installations the next day. Besides, having had a stressful day, he will be unproductive if he decides to work through the night. Judy is stressed out as well. But before they catch a taxi, they amble along the walkway, talking.

"So, you're getting back to your works, right?" Judy asks.

"Yeah," Garret answers.

"How long is it gonna take?"

"I don't know. I just have to keep trying different ways to get a single streak. I feel there is just one piece of the formula that is missing – it appears to be the blockade in the whole experiment. I try to work it out theoretically – you know, some calculations and stuff, but I still don't quite get it. I thought my formula was complete. But I think there might be a piece of the puzzle missing."

"Do you think you might be pushing yourself too hard?"

"Nah, I don't think so…"

"Well, I learnt that some of these experiments can be very stubborn in the beginning, especially if you keep getting a particular result that you cannot explain. It just makes you sick and somewhat desperate – so bad that you end up abandoning the whole project eventually."

"No, not this one. This particular project was my thesis for my master's degree program back at the NRL. I want to make sure I get it right. It'll give me the feeling that I actually completed the program and obtained my master's degree."

"Where did you go to school before your time at the NRL? The Naval Academy?" Judy questions, with a fold across her forehead.

"Yeah."

"Oh… (scratches her hair) Daniel told me you joined the lab from there. What happened? Why did you not continue with them?"

"It's a long story…"

"You can make it short."

"Uh… can we not talk about this, please?"

"Sorry," Judy whispers and makes the zip-up sign across her lips.

They walk on, waiting for who will raise the next topic between them. Garret, however, does not like the fact that Daniel told her that he came from the Navy. It gives room for more questions – questions that will resurface the memories he's been trying to forget.

"So tell me: are you married or you got a girlfriend?" Judy finally breaks the awkward silence.

"Neither… haven't really had the time for courtship. It's been all about school and work."

"That's nerdy."

Garret chuckles.

"No, it's not. You know when you're pretty hooked up with something – it just seems like nothing else matters… *But then you end up getting a dishonorable discharge.*"

His voice fades off to silence and the last words are said in his mind.

"So you've not had the hots for any lady?"

"Not really – I had casual friends at school – nothing beyond platonic…"

The conversation stretches through a distance. It is a moment to be completely taken away from the confines of science to his personal life, and Garret is quite enjoying it. But for what awaits him at home, he has no idea – even though he always appears ready for anything at any time.

Garret has the taxi stop a block away from his house, it's almost 8pm. He journeys along the street, toward his residents. It is faintly lighted here – not all the streetlamps are working – some parts of street are dark.

Garret has his bag in his hand as he marches along. The trees spread a shadow on both sides of the road from the moon. His searching eyes move suspiciously in every direction. There's a feeling that he is being followed. His house is No.7 – he has just walked past No.3.

He hears a shuffling somewhere – but he is not sure where it is. It seemed like it came from the large oak tree nearby. The feeling is stronger now. He stops and looks in the direction. The area around this particular tree is shaded with moon light. Garret keeps his eyes at the tree while his ears listen out for movements.

But as he did not hear or see anything, he continues on his way. Whoever it is should be bold enough to face him. Sadly, thugs don't make themselves known, he thinks.

Finally, he gets to his house. As he enters the walkway, he hears another shuffling – this time, behind the flowerbed at the right corner of his house. A shadow appears to flash across his eyes. He stops in his tracks – eyes wheeling about in their sockets. The shuffling is only for a split second, almost the same as the shadow movement. Garret changes course toward the flowerbed, but continues to look back all the while.

Unfortunately, he finds no one around the flowerbed. He scans the whole place and then heads to the backyard. There are more flowerbeds and shrubs here – hiding spots for whoever or whatever it is. Garret goes behind each of them, but finds no one.

Through the left side of the house, he returns to the front door. For now, it feels like the whole place is safe. It could be paranoia after all. Even so, he looks around one more time – it's all still – the silence is only broken by the barking of a neighbor's dog.

It may all seem calm, but Garret knows someone is keeping an eye on him – the feeling is too strong to ignore. He would have thought it was Ziko if they had not done business together since the first time he saw him glaring at him from his car. However, the possibility that it could be him is not entirely ruled out. But if not Ziko, then who could be keeping tabs on him, and for what reason? Far be it that it is a spy assigned by his principal officers in the Navy. He's been dismissed and they have no business with him anymore. The thoughts will keep him cautious of his surroundings until the feeling fades away or whoever is watching him reveals himself.

CHAPTER SEVEN: YES! YES! YES!

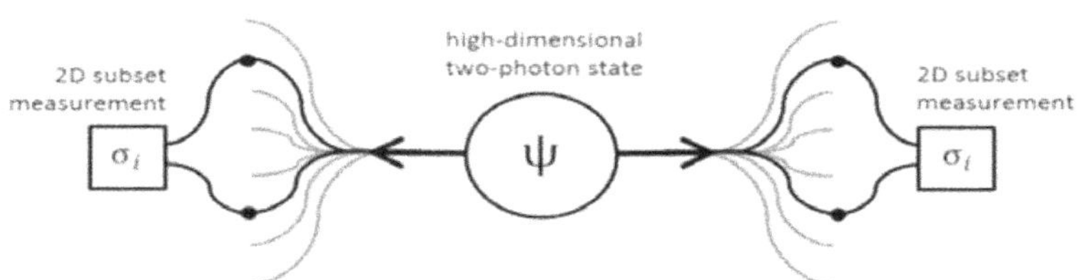

The facilities from Allied Corporations have been delivered and installed. Barnes' Laboratory has been expanded to fit in the pieces of equipment. They, including those from the used market and Logan's Photonics have been tested and are all working fine. All pieces of equipment have been integrated. Garret and even Barny can't be more excited. He has all he needs, and tonight, he resumes his experiment.

Garret is in Barny's office to discuss the theory and formula behind the teleportation project. They try to keep it low so as not to alert the others of this top secret project.

"Teleportation is the transfer of matter or energy. It may be hypothetical, but the fact that it happened in that accident proves that it is possible," Garret says.

Barny moves closer and rests his hands on the table, looking Garret in the eyes.

"In quantum teleportation, matter is not transferred from one point to another, but information is. So how do you intend to transfer matter or energy between two different points?"

"I am not entirely sure, but I am thinking that if I can combine transmission of classical information and the quantum energy fluctuations, maybe I'll be able to teleport an object no matter how small or how big. Think about it, Barny: it could not have been the increased strength of the laser beam. There's definitely a fluctuation in the vacuum state of the quantum field that existed around the confocal system at the time."

"So what you're saying is that you want to exploit the quantum energy fluctuations in the quantum field?"

"That's what I think."

"And how do you transmit classical information – through the laser beam of energy?"

"It could be through laser wave communication. It is similar to radio waves. Laser waves have never been proven and are still a theory on paper."

There seems to be sense in what Garret is saying, Barny thinks. The fluctuations in the energy could agitate the material compound of an object, and with the laser energy focused on it, they could achieve teleportation.

"I see you're working with Judy," Barny intones.

"Uh… yeah, but that's for the other project – not this one."

"Okay…"

At night, Garret is in the lab, alone. Judy has somewhere else to be at the time so she left early. Garret has worked out the theoretical aspect of the teleportation project on his computer. It is time to make it practical.

He will have to start with a tiny sample – one that is of low density and compactness. He goes to the Prototyping Clean Room. He makes sure that Judy is not in there, before going in. Looking through the room, he can't find what he wants. Garret reaches in his pocket and pulls out his dad's military coin that was given to him for flying his hundredth mission in Vietnam.

Garret returns to the workroom. He carefully holds up the coin with a long pair of lab forceps. The coin is placed in the portal of the processor. Garret turns on the RF Transmitter which is connected to the LaserBoxx Series. He programs the wavelength on the RF Transmitter as to the distance and location – based on GPS monitoring system. The Flux Variant is also connected to the Series. It is turned on. A high-pitch sound blares in the Series. It is the process of excitation of the beam that is about to be projected on the sample.

The sound continues so high that Garret has to plug his ears with his IPods to block it off – even so, he can still hear it ringing in his head.

Garret raises the frequency of the beam with the beam expander. His eyes are already hidden behind the eye trackers. And finally, the sample is bombarded with the laser beam. As it shoots out from the Series, the high-pitch sound begins to subside.

With everything set and working fine, Garret watches as the beam carrying the laser wave interacts with the military coin. As revealed by his X-ray crystallography, there is a free atom circulating around the coin. The computer data is showing that there is a magnetic field around the free atom. The Flux Variant is expected to increase the magnetic field and with the quantum computer and other equipment, a quantum field is being created around the sample. With the look of curiosity and expectancy on the face of Garret, this is probably what he is occurring.

Garret looks through the objective lens of the portal and discovers that the coin is glowing green – there are also tiny sparks and circular waves of light spinning around the coin. But nothing is happening to the material component of the coin. However, he notices that the core of the coin is hollow. There could be some degree of dematerialization going on. He keeps his eyes on the lens, hoping that this hollow part will expand.

But after a couple of minutes, the hollow part neither widens nor closes up. Garret stands back, exhales deeply and stares at the computer and all the data that is running down the screen. He did everything right. The Flux Variant was well adjusted. What did he not do right? He thinks while reviewing the computer data.

He decides to repeat the process, adjusting the level of every piece of equipment. He repositions the sample and makes sure the beam stabilizer is in place. He also adjusts the Flux Variant – maybe it will provide enough magnetic field and in turn the quantum field to bring about the dematerialization of the sample.

Unfortunately, the beam only penetrates the coin, agitates the atoms, but does not cause any kind of dematerialization. Upon looking through the portal, Garret sees the hollow part of the coin. Just as before, it is neither getting wider nor smaller.

Garret pours a deep breath – hands on his waist. He is confused, having done everything still not getting the desired result. Maybe he will have to revisit his theoretical plan – there could be something he is missing. The fact that he is able to create a hole within the atoms of the molecule means he could be getting somewhere. And he is sure that this hole is not that formed by the material of the coin itself…

He continues to work on the project until dawn. And when Judy and the other workers at the lab come to work in the morning, he switches to the original experiment.

However, at 10am, he is in Barny's office to report the outcome of the experiment.

"I see you worked all night," Barny observes how heavy his eyes are.

"Yes sir. And I was able to create a hole within the atoms of the material – although the rest of the compound remained intact."

"Did you check the frequency of the beam – did you try to increase wave length?"

"Yes, I did. I also tried to adjust the flux density to create a stronger magnetic and quantum field, but it didn't work. I also adjusted the angle of bombardment. But I think I need to make some calculations. Perhaps the magnetic field will have to work in line with the components of the sample – that and some other factors, I intend work on tonight. I've switched to the original experiment already."

Barny sighs and reclines on his chair. He seems to already see the success in the project – but perhaps it is due to his belief in Garret.

"The first time you observed the teleportation, it was with a bio sample, right?" he asks.

"It was," Garret replies.

"How about you try it again, using the same sample?"

Garret gives it a quick consideration and nods.

"You may be right. It's probably easy for the laser to penetrate a less compact sample. I could work with that."

Barny scratches his chin and glances through his glass door.

"What about Judy? I observe she wants to be a part of the experiment," he asks.

"Yeah, she wants to. But I want to keep this is classified as possible, at least until I get it right."

"But she's working with you in the original experiment."

"Yes, she is. I didn't have a choice."

"She's pretty intelligent. She will make a good assistant."

"No doubt about that…"

Garret might work with Judy later, but for now, he is all about completing the teleportation experiment.

However, Judy has some work to do at the Nanoprototyping Room while Garret works on the original experiment. He had gone to the room to collect a sample and had met her while she was performing test on other experiments.

"You've started working on your experiment, right?" she asked.

"About to start," Garret answered. "Guess you're too busy to join me."

"Yeah. I will be done here shortly…"

And now, Garret is in the lab. The tiny sample has been placed on the slide of the confocal system and set between the pieces of laser tubes. The photon counter and the micropositioners are in place. It could have been possible that the systems got agitated when Garret increased the frequency of the laser. This time, he will have to work with the recommended frequency.

He projects the light toward the sample, and makes the necessary adjustments on the computer. With his eyes hidden behind the eye tracker once again, he watches the interaction between the light and the sample through the portal of the machine.

The sample only absorbs small photons of light and electrons are ejected out of its surface. But the electrons ejected, even when the sample has been cooled below absolute zero temperature, are not enough to cause the necessary reactions.

Garret may fear that if he increases the frequency of the laser, it might cause the same damage as in the NRL. But according to classical physics, he understands that there is no limit to the amount of frequency when working with a sample below absolute zero. So maybe the best is to reduce the intensity of the light, and then increase the frequency electrical waves.

Unfortunately, the desired result is far from which after he applied the theory. He sits back and tries different theories on his computer, yet nothing works. He projects an X-ray at the bio sample – it only provides the original result as in the days of W.C. Rontgen. It's either the experiment is not feasible on its own, or he is not doing it correctly. Garret wonders how long it would have taken him to achieve the expected result if he was still conducting the experiment in the NRL – after all, having sophisticated facilities is no longer the problem.

However, Garret does not give up. Through the whole day, he continues to tweak his formula and come up with different theories. Even after each of the theories fail, he continues to try. But through it all, he doesn't quite get it right.

"Maybe leaving it for now is the best," Judy advises. "Maybe going out and doing other things will clear your mind. The agitation is written all over you."

Garret thinks the advice a reasonable one. He has to go out and work with the others to clear his head – not actually for the original experiment, but the teleportation project. He hopes to get it right this time.

***

At night, Garret returns to the teleportation experiment. This time, he is to work with a bio sample as Mr. Barnes advised. It has been collected and held up between the cameras and photon counter. He turns on the RF transmitter connected to the LaserBoxx Series and programs the electrical wavelength. The Flux Variant connected to the Series is turned on. The frequency of the laser is increased. The computer is absorbing all the data.

Now he watches from behind the eye tracker as the beam bearing the radio information hit the sample. But even though the molecules that make up the piece of bone is not so compact, there is still no dematerialization. The bone behaves as though it is bombarded by an X-ray.

Garret tries again and again, but nothing works. He suspends a sample of the coin, hoping that something will happen this time. With all the systems connected and the beam hitting the sample, the result remains the same.

Garret takes a deep breath and leans against the table behind. He has tried all he can for now, yet he is unable to get the expected result.

"What could be wrong," he mutters to himself.

Not only are the samples below absolute zero temperature, they absorb the laser in the right order and spectrum. The systems are all working fine. The interaction between the sample and the light is right on the spot. The electrons ejected on the surface of the sample are energetic enough, showing that the light under the right wavelength and frequency is well absorbed. So what exactly is the problem?

Garret looks around the lab – the systems stare back at him. Maybe they have something to tell him – if only they could. But somewhere near the door is a table, on top of which are some books. Maybe they will tell him something he does not know already – or something he has forgotten.

He goes to the bookshelf and pulls one of Einstein's quantum theory books down. He flips through the pages, focusing on the part that explains quantum experiment. But he finds nothing new – he has carefully followed every detail in the book. He opens another of Einstein's books and glances through the pages – and then another – and another. None of the books provides an escape to this deadlock he's experiencing.

He leans against the table, looking at everything in the lab – from the coffee mug on a small desk nearby, to the quantum computer, and to the confocal system. He pours out a breath – there seems to be nothing left to try.

"Wait, the coffee mug!" he exclaims. And then he bursts into laughter. He thinks it is a bizarre thought to use a coffee mug as a sample – as big as it is and at room temperature.

"You're such an idiot, Garret." He continues to laugh at himself. Desperate times go with desperate measures. He just wants to make the teleportation experiment possible. There's a reason as to why it happened during his original experiment. It could have been by accident, but now he believes it can be achieved.

His laughter finally reduces to a smile. He coughs lightly and sets his eyes on the mug. A giggle escapes him. There's zero possibility of the mug standing in as the working sample. Garret is convinced it doesn't possess the qualities of a pure sample.

He giggles again and goes over to the table where the mug is. He picks it up and turns it over in his hands, with criticism in his smile. Maybe if the cup could talk, it would ask him to get his hands off it – the insults are starting to get on its nerves. But even as Garret thinks it's stupid to try out the coffee mug, something keeps pushing him to it. Made with glazed ceramic or some other material, the mug could possess some properties that will react with the laser energy and give the expected result.

"There's no harm in trying," Garret tells himself.

He raises the mug and looks at it closely. A second thought smolders into his head.

"Don't be stupid, Garret – it's not gonna work."

He puts down the cup. It's pointless that a ceramic mug would give the expected result. And there is no way he can suspend the whole mug as a sample.

He shifts his eyes between the confocal system and the mug. The need to try something new, no matter how weird it is, surpasses the reluctance to break the mug.

"Are you my hero," he says to the mug.

He takes the ceramic mug to the confocal system. Garret sets the sample up. He turns the systems back on. The laser beam carrying the distance and coordinates through radio communication is projected on the sample. Garret is still not sure where he is headed. How foolish he will think of himself if this does not work! There's already a lot of doubt in his mind, even as he carries on with the experiment.

Wearing the eye tracker back on, he watches the laser interact with the sample. The light penetrates the molecules of the mug, producing a dark green glow within. Gradually, the light spreads and takes over the whole mug. Garret no longer sees the mug, but a tiny cloud of dark green light starts swirling around the mug within moments millions of what seems to be clouds of sparks appear. The cloud lingers on for a while and then disappears. Garret can feel his heart thumping with excitement. But he wants to be sure of what is happening or has happened.

He looks closely between in the portal of the machine. The sample is no longer there. He takes off the eye tracker and looks closely again with his naked eyes. He does not see anything. His eyelids are fluttering. His face is turning crimson. The sample had been directed by the GPS coordinates set to the table in Mr. Barnes' office. Now Garret backs away from the equipment and runs through the door down the hall to Barny's office.

He dashes straight in the office. Luckily, it is unlocked. He goes through. According to the coordinates, the sample is supposed to land at the corner of the desk.

Garret walks slowly to it – there is the ceramic coffee mug sitting on the corner of Barny's desk. His whole body is shaking at this point. He walks closer and picks it up. He stares at it to be sure it is the same mug. The corners of his mouth are spreading into a wide smile. His hands are still shaking, and with that come the eruption:

"YES! YES! YES!"

He dashes out of Mr. Barnes' office and runs around the lab, yelling: "It works – it works…" The exhilaration is real. Even if he tries again and it doesn't work, there is hope of success now. He will only continue to try again and again, applying the same theories and principles.

Garret returns to the room holding the coffee mug in his hand. Now he stares at it and the lab equipment. There is more to do, he thinks. He will have to experiment on a bigger sample – maybe the several mugs this time. He no longer thinks it is foolish to use the mug as a sample. If it works, then he has achieved what has never been done in the world of physics. If it doesn't, he will still regard himself as a hero of 'small success'.

He goes back to Mr. Barnes office and gets another coffee mug. He took the mug from his table and hopes to send it back there through teleportation.

He places two coffee mugs inside the portal and powers on the systems again, adjusting the radio communication to the right GPS coordinates. Since the samples are larger, it means it has more molecules to take up with the light energy. And that means turning up the frequency, wavelength and intensity of the laser waves a little bit.

He applies all the computer data into the system and puts on his eye tracker. Once again, the light meets the samples. Gradually, the molecules that make up the mug begin to absorb the circulating light. Garret watches as this absorption spreads throughout the mug, forming a dark green cloud of sparkling lights. The whole process takes less than a 10 seconds. And then suddenly, the mugs disappear.

Garret beams as he makes his way to Mr. Barnes' office. He has not been this happy in a long time. But of course he has every right to be happy. As little as it may seem, he is proud of himself.

His jaw drops as he opens the door to Mr. Barnes' office to find the mugs right on his desk. Garret's chest is rising and falling as his excitement reaches the peak. He pads closer and grabs the mugs slowly as if it would shatter if he grabbed it too fast. He turns them over in his hand, admiring it. That feeling of accomplishment washes over him. At long last, he has achieved something as a solo scientist. All those sleepless nights are not in vain after all. His life's savings and those of Barny's are not poured into an empty basket. He can't wait to share the news with Barny.

But before he calls Barny, he downloads all the critical data and finalizes his formula and stores the information on his laptop.

He reaches forth to the telephone and dials his number, still admiring one of the mugs. It is late. Barny will be sleeping at this time. But Garret wants him to be the first to come to the lab at dawn.

"This better be important, boy," Barny warns in a sleepy tone.

"I can assure you it is…"

"Hold on! Let me guess: you've achieved…"

"Success in the teleportation experiment, YES!" Garret completes his words excitedly. "I can teleport a coffee mug to your office. I also teleported two mugs on my second try…. It's so beautiful…"

"Say no more… I'm right on my way. This is a lot to take in…"

Barny ends the call. Garret goes and drops himself on Barny's chair and then swivels it. As he rolls about, he spreads his hands in the air, holding the mug. Having worked so hard for this, he has every reason to be happy with his success. Barny will be the first person he will demonstrate his success to. But it shouldn't just be the coffee mug. He has to try out other objects, and he has to send them to other locations too.

Garret takes a couple of deep breaths. His eyes narrow down. He has realized that his success is not complete yet.

He goes to the Clean Room for a different sample – a live mouse. Maybe the fur and skin and other parts that make up the mouse will absorb the laser and dematerialize everything, including the bones to an energy pattern. Maybe it will work that way instead of just bombarding a piece of bone with the laser.

However, the experiment is not successful as Garret works on it. He tries again and again, but the laser only penetrates the skin, behaving somewhat like an X-ray. Garret understands that the experiment is only successful with nonliving objects.

He goes ahead to try other objects – books, lab utensils, objects made of glass – one of which is the glass prism, objects made of plastic – like the telephone, stapler, tape dispenser and more.

One basic fact Garret understands is that: for now, the experiment works with objects the same size as the coffee mug, or a little bigger because of the size of the portal. If he wanted to teleport larger items, he'll need to build a larger portal system. He can teleport objects anywhere around the lab. He is however, yet to decipher how far objects can be teleported.

He has just sent an empty aerosol can outside the building. He goes out to find it, when Barny's car pulls over in the parking space. Garret locates the can next to a robotic trolley outside, and then walks toward Barny's car.

"What do we have here, son?" Barny speaks first, coming toward him, with a wide smile on his face.

"Something amazing!" Garret replies in the same parlance, beaming from ear to ear.

"An aerosol can too?" Barny observes.

"We're only faced with not being able to teleport living organisms and objects larger than this (raising the can). And at this time I'm not sure how far the objects can travel."

Barny takes the can from him and admires it. The smile has reduced to one side of his mouth.

"Come and show me," he tells Garret.

"Let's do it – come on."

They both walk through the door to the lab, chatting all the while. Garret now leads the way to the lab, convinced that his first demonstration will be a success.

"Whoa, what a mess you made here!" Barny comments upon seeing all the printed out sheets of data spread across the table and floor.

"Yeah. There is a lot of data to analyze."

Garret leads him closer to the confocal system. He has the mug in his hand, and a face glowing with enthusiasm.

"Now let's start with the coffee mug," he declares.

Barny stands by as Garret sets up the experiment. The mug is placed in the portal, the systems are turned back on. In a short time, the laser meets the mug. The interaction that follows produces the dark green circular cloud of sparkling light. Barny tries not to blink. Maybe if he had, he would have missed the mug vanishing from between the portal.

"This is incredible!" he remarks.

"Come on, let's go get it." Garret's face is still lit up with smile.

Barny follows him to his office, where the mug now rests on his desk. His face turns pale with astonishment. His mouth falls slightly open as he gazes at the mug.

"This is amazing, son. You have broken the boundaries of quantum physics – in fact, physics generally. This is something that has never been achieved – not even by the scientists before us – not even by Einstein himself. This is wonderful…"

He walks further to the table and takes the mug. He presses it hard between his hands, as if trying to break it. But the mug remains unyielding.

"The properties remain the same. It has neither lost its density nor become too fragile. I don't wanna say this is unbelievable because it is. Come here…"

The corners of Garret's eyes crinkle as he moves to where Barny is with a smile. Barny wraps him in an embrace like his biological father did.

"Congratulations, son." Barny withdraws from the hug, but still has his hands on Garret's shoulders, looking into his eyes. "You have made me so proud. This is a ground-breaking invention, and we must secure it."

"Thank you. I couldn't have achieved it without your help," Garret replies. "You've been supportive from day one. You've always believed in me. I dedicate this success to you, Barny. Thank you for all you've done for me."

"Let's not think about that, son – there are still a lot that needs to be done…"

Garret breaks off the moment and limps to his chair. Garret sits opposite him, trying to calm the rhapsody of excitement going on inside of him.

"We will have to decipher how far we can teleport an object. We have to make the systems portable – and for that, we will have to make another custom micro-domitor with other components built into it. And we have to keep this away from everyone else until the job is done. You understand?"

"Yes, Barny. I already made research about the portable custom micro-domitor with all the necessary components embedded in it. It's in the market. I will have to contact Ziko for parts."

"Don't you think he might find out that you've completed the experiment?" Barny's brows snap together.

"I don't think so. And I doubt he knows exactly what I have been working on."

"How about you talk directly with the suppliers? Or maybe contact the CEO of Allied Corporations. I think the latter will be better. They will surely have what you need."

"Come on, Barny, you and I know how expensive an all-in-one system like that will be, especially when it is bought from the retail market."

Barny sighs and leans closer to the table – eyes set at Garret.

"Let's make it happen. I'll support you with whatever you have…"

"No, no, no, Barny; you've done enough already," Garret protests – inadmissible lines draw across his forehead. "I don't think this is right…"

"Well, I think it is," Barny cuts in. "Listen to me, son: ever since I became a scientist and worked at the NRL, I have tried to achieve something as a scientist. I have tried to come up with a ground-breaking invention. I have worked with different aims, different samples. I may have achieved one or two inventions, but none of that can be compared to this. And that is why I am most grateful to you for bringing me into this project. I will do whatever I can to make it work, even if I have to sell this place…"

"NEVER!"

"Don't interrupt me, son! That's what scientists do; we make sacrifices for our projects, even when we are not entirely sure of success. Now talk about one that is already successful…"

He turns the mug around on the table as if to strengthen his resolution. Now he reclines on the chair, with his hand on the table.

"That Ziko guy looks dangerous to me. He's cunning. He will surely understand that the experiment is complete. You might be surprised he already knows what you're working on. I think we should get this custom-built system from Allied Corporation."

Garret also thinks Ziko is a dangerous man. With the remarks he had made and the effort he put in to make sure he got all the facilities needed without asking for anything, Garret needs not be told that there's something fishy about him.

"I think getting it from the retail market is the best," he agrees. "But…"

"But what?"

"The money…Barny, it'll be selfish of me to…"

"Let's not talk further about this, Garret." Barny's jaw tightens.

Garret falls silent at once. He knows, nonetheless, that Barny is only feigning anger so he can change the topic. And that is clear because Barny has a smile hovering around his lips even when he tries to keep a straight countenance.

"You know that doesn't look good on you," Garret teases.

The corners of his mouth finally break apart with the smile. Garret takes a deep breath and relaxes on the chair.

"Wait, have you experimented on materials in their liquid and gaseous states – even in powdery form?" Barny inquires.

"Yes. But they will have to be contained in a can or a paper or a cellophane bag or even glass – just any container about the size of the coffee mug."

"So all we are left to do now is to find out how far we can send objects?"

"Yes."

"All right…" Barny looks around his office as if searching for something, but then his eyes fall back on Garret. "You will have to contact the Allied Corporations and place an order…"

Yes, Garret will contact Allied Corporations. He will. And they will deliver the custom, all-in-one system. Garret sure knows that his name is now in the history books. He has achieved the impossible, by sheer brilliance and consistency. Thanks to the advancement of science and technology, Garret has put his knowledge and that of other scientists together to achieve what will be regarded as one of the greatest discoveries of all time. And when this discovery is demonstrated before the eyes of thousands, if not millions of people, the world will appreciate his brilliance. But the glory, he believes is not for him alone, but for Barny as well. They will both demonstrate this great advancement of science to the world.

CHAPTER EIGHT: T-SYSTEM

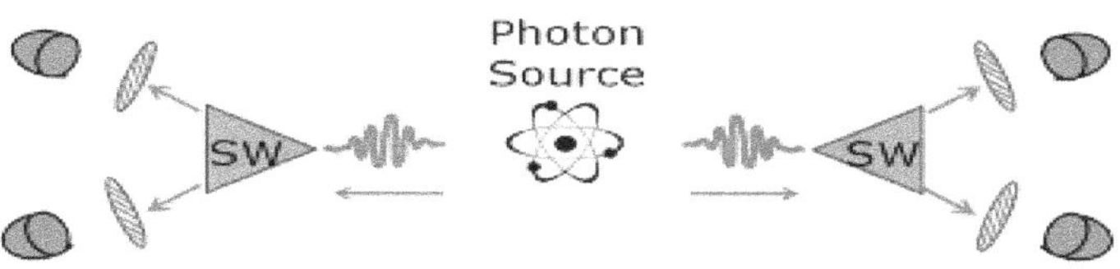

There was no point delaying. The order was made in the day. Garret specifically asked that the system be delivered at night. This was to make sure that none of the other workers at the lab know about the delivery. Barny stayed with Garret through hours into the night to test the system and fine-tune his formula.

The custom system came in the shape of a rectangular box the size of a small kitchen mirowave. It has several components built in one piece – the micro-domitor, micropositioners, beam expander, quantum processor, FX Laser Jet and the portal expander. It is one of a kind. And acquiring it reduced both Garret's and Barny's accounts to absolute zero along with a larger bank lean on Barnes Laboratory. But they were both glad they bought it as an asset for the laboratory.

"It should be called 'T-system," Garret told Barny.

"And what does the 'T' mean?" asked Barny.

"'Teleport' – 'Teleport-system'."

Barny purses his lips and nods. "Not bad," he agrees.

The T-system could be transported in a large wooden chest and stored in Barny's office. But Garret is considering taking it to somewhere safer. Following his encounter with Norman, he doesn't think the laboratory is the safest place for the T-system – he doesn't even consider his home safe. And he is yet to find a place for it. Until he does, the system remains in the lab.

Garret plods through the walkway to his house, with his bag containing his laptop hanging down his shoulder. He's had an arduous day. With the shadow beneath his puffy eyes, his body yearns for a good night's sleep. He will just settle for some snacks, have his shower and dive into bed.

The silver hinges grate and he walks through the door. His hands grope across the wall for the switch.

Found it! He switches on the light. And as soon as his eyes get accustomed to the bright lights, he finds a middle-aged man sitting comfortably in his couch. He is of a regular physique and wearing a black suit. Garret is not intimidated by the intense gaze in his eyes. He is only startled by the sudden sight of him.

"Hello Garret," he greets - the corners of his mouth breaking into a mischievous smile.

"Who the hell you, and how did you get in here?" Garret huffs, standing by the door and glaring hard at this man.

"My name is Agent Norman - from the CIA."

"From the what?" Garret's face scrunches up.

What is a CIA agent doing in his house – worst of all, sneaking in?

"How did you get in here?" he storms.

"You don't expect me to answer that – do you?"

"Hell yeah, I do!"

"Well I just found my way in. Come on, Garret – why don't you sit down and let's discuss something more important?"

"You don't order me around in my house..."

"Suit yourself then..."

There's silence between them now – for a brief minute while.

"We know all about your project, and we've been following you. We found out that you have achieved great success. It is for this reason that I am here. It's quite too early, right? Yeah, I know. But seeing how great your discovery is, we had to make sure we talk to you first about it, before anyone else does..."

"What project? What discovery are you talking about?" Garret feigns ignorance.

"You know what I'm talking about – the teleportation project. We know you have been able to teleport small objects like a coffee mug. I must say it's amazing. I mean, it's something that has never been achieved, despite several trials. Congratulations for that...!"

"I don't know what you're talking about. And right now, I'll ask that you leave my house."

Norman sighs and gets on his feet, adjusting his suit. With wild eyes and hardened jaw, Garret glares at him.

"You have been invited to the office of the CIA Director. He wants to have a word with you. I'll advice you honor the invitation."

"And if I don't?" Garret's eyes grow even wilder.

"Just honor the invitation – it's pointless making threats now. Good night, Garret."

He pulls on his suit once again and leaves through the door. Garret slams the door shut but watches through the window as Agent Norman marches down the walkway.

He wonders how the CIA found out that he was working on an experiment. It could not have been from the Navy - they have no idea of the teleportation project. No one else knows about the project except...

The curtain is drawn as Garret takes his hand off it. Norman has gone out of sight at this time.

"Could it be Ziko?" Garret murmurs – brows snapping together.

Maybe it's him. Maybe he's an agent for the CIA. No wonder he helped him acquire the pieces of equipment from the foreign marketers, without asking for anything in return. But how did he know that the experiment is successful and that he is able to teleport a coffee mug and other objects? Only I, and Mr. Barnes know about that. Or could it have slipped from Mr. Barnes to someone else - maybe Daniel or George or Judy.

"No, I don't think Barny will do that. No-way," he mutters.

But there has to be a way the CIA found out. One thing is for sure: the T-system is not safe. Maybe they're tapping into the conversations at the lab, or maybe even have a secret camera somewhere. It has to be. That's the only explanation to how they 'have been following up', according to Norman.

Garret wants to call Barny and tell him about what just happened. But he decides otherwise. His house might be bugged with CIA electronics. Garret will have to wait to see Barney tomorrow in the lab.

***

The day came with its own demands. There was a delivery to make, and so all hands were on deck to make sure the equipment was fixed and delivered. Garret and Barny were to make the delivery and installation.

The job has been done - and now they both make their way back to the labs loading dock.

Garret has told Barny about his encounter with Agent Norman.

"I mean; how did they know about the experiment? How did they know that it was successful?" He ends his narration with the questions.

"I don't know. I believe the CIA just has their way of finding out about something," Barny answers - arms stretched on the steering.

Garret breathes out and adjusts his bottom on the chair.

"Well I don't care however they found out. I am not honoring the invitation..."

"Yes, you will - you have to," Barny cuts in. "You have to go to find out what they want. You must understand that you are now in high demand. You have created something that has never been seen in the history of science - only seen on the TV show, Star Trek. You must understand that there will be lots of people calling for your attention now... this is the most amazing scientific breakthrough civilization has ever seen"

"I know, Barny - I know. But the government spying on us? Isn't it wrong? Don't they need a warrant or something to be doing that"?

"You think someone is selling you out?" Barny glances at him.

"I don't know what to think anymore. Could someone be listening to our conversations?" Lines grew between Garret's brows.

"I don't know who? Maybe Ziko could be keeping tabs on you - who knows? But I don't really think you should set your mind at that now. I suggest you honor the invitation. You might get the answers to your questions from the CIA..."

Garret knows there's a point in what Barny is saying, but he still thinks it's not worth it. He can find out how the CIA got to know about the completed experiment himself. He must not honor their invitation to get that piece of information. He doesn't trust the government. It always has a way of forcing someone to give up their most-prized possession and then take the credit. Garret wants something better for his hard work. Going to the CIA will only open compromises – and that, he doesn't want.

It is just like every other day at the laboratory – exhausting. At the hour of 7, the taxi pulls over at the entrance to Garret's street. He slams the taxis door behind him.

With his computer bag hanging down his shoulder, he trudges to his house. But then, there's a feeling that someone is on his track. He stops looks back, but finds no one. His eyes explore the area. The trees on both sides of the road cast a dark shadow behind them. The lights along the street only give a faint exposition, just like the moonlight. There's not much detail to gather – but the feeling lingers.

Garret slows down his step, looking around. It's like someone is waiting for him to make the wrong move so they can pounce on him. And now, the feeling is getting stronger.

Garret halts his movement. Behind the trees there seem like a thousand eyes skulking. If only he could see through to confirm his suspicion. It is not paranoia. It is not because Norman visited and he feels the CIA have their eyes on him. Someone is definitely hiding somewhere.

"Who's there?" Garret calls out.

The only voice he hears is his expressing caution and readiness. And as the silence returns, only broken by the buzzing of nocturnal insects, he continues on his way home.

But he suddenly hears the thumping of footsteps behind him. He turns sharply, but his head is smiting with a huge object. He drops to the ground and fades.

***

Garret stirs and opens his eyes slowly. It's blurry at first, but gradually, his eyes get accustomed to the thin lights. Two men are standing over him. Their thick, broad chests and shoulders swell and bounce as they crack their knuckles. With full beard across their jaws and thick cheek bones, their faces are intimidating enough to make a sissy wet his pants. But even as they glare down at Garret with their hooded, hazel eyes, there's not a hint of fear in him.

The men's eyes follow him as he scrambles to a sitting position, looking around. If keeping a close watch on him is so he doesn't escape, then the men may actually be the ones that fear him. There are other thugs standing in strategic positions around the warehouse – about four of them. It seems impossible that Garret will defeat all of them and escape.

But even as Garret's eyes go around the warehouse, they fall on the man sitting on a couch about two yards away – Ziko. He is dressed in thick leather jacket. In his hand is a baton – he continues to fling it and twirl it about. Two other thugs are standing on both sides of the chair – their faces as rocky as those of the others.

Garret shuffles to his feet and glares at the two men beside him – they both return the favor. Rubbing the back of his head where he was hit, he walks toward Ziko.

"Hello friend, you're awake!" Ziko intones, with a smile of mischief lined across his thin face.

"It was you? You sent one of these bastards to attack me?" Garret questions – his brows snapping together.

"Words, boy; words."

"Screw that!" Garret flares. "You dare send one of these Bozos to attack me…" the men move to attack him again, but Ziko raises his

109

hand – they all stand back. "…and you still want me to choose my words carefully?"

Ziko flings the baton in his hand as if to reveal to Garret that it was the weapon they used on him.

"You would have ignored my invitation if I had asked nicely. Besides, I wanted to send a message…"

"What message was that?"

Ziko widens his smile, and glances up at the thug on his right who has no room for smile on his own face. He gets on his feet and swaggers closer to Garret.

"If only you knew the kind of man standing in front of you, you will filter your words…" he is standing a few inches away from Garret, looking deep into his eyes. Garret's eyes, wild and hazel, show no sign of being intimidated. "We are not here to make threats…" he takes some steps backwards. "In fact, we are here to reach an agreement…" now he goes back and sits on the chair.

Garret was going to ask: 'what agreement was that?', but he has gained control of his emotions. Now he glares at Ziko, rubbing the back of his head at intervals.

"I must congratulate you for discovering the art of teleportation," Ziko continues. "Trust me, I am the happiest man on earth right now – and that is why I am putting up with your attitude…"

"What are you talking about?" Garret's eyes furrow again.

"Ah, there he goes. Of course you know what I'm talking about. You have become the first scientist to practically teleport an object from one point to another. This is not Star Trek or some sci-fi book – this is for real. You did not invent new equipment for it. But with a gathering of already-existing pieces of equipment, you created a formula and made one of the greatest discoveries of all time. I gotta say you're one hell of a genius."

Garret has had enough. He storms to where he is sitting – the thugs are shuffling their feet, thinking he is coming for a fight.

"I do not know what you're talking about. And if this is the reason you brought me here, then I have to go now."

He turns back and storms toward the exit. Two of the men stand in his way, but he flings a massive right hand across one of their faces. The thug that is hit staggers backward as his eyes disperse the twinkles. The other thug fires a punch toward Garret's face. But Garret catches it and delivers a swift punch to his neck. He falls backward, choking and coughing. The other men move in immediately and surround Garret. He glances from one to another, ready to take on all of them.

"The temper!" Ziko yells from behind. "How did you tolerate all that training at the Navy?"

"Why don't you come closer and find out, you sucker?" Garret spits.

"On the contrary, you will have to find out that this is not the Navy. This is street – and right here, I run the show."

Immediately he dropped the last word, his men swoop in on Garret. One of them tries to attack from the right, but Garret already sees him and delivers an elbow around his lower jaw. At the same time, the man on the left grabs Garret's left hand. He tries to fight free, but one of the men that were standing over him when he woke up attacks from behind, smacking Garret so hard that he falls on his face. The others rush in and begin to punch and kick him while he is on the ground. Garret tries to defend himself as much as he can, but the men have him overpowered.

They continue to beat him for a moment until Ziko raises his hand.

"That's enough, guys!" he warns. "That's not a good way to treat our guest."

The men withdraw from Garret, cracking their knuckles, and glaring down at him – chests rising and falling heavily. Garret winces and growls in pain. His lips are broken. He spits out the blood in his mouth, coughing lightly.

"I'm so sorry, Garret," Ziko apologizes, standing over him. "It was not my intention that this meeting would go this way. But it's not my fault. You're making it difficult for us to reach an understanding." He turns to his men. "Get him up. And tie his hands"

The men pull Garret up, securing his hands tightly behind him. His breathing hard – his face scowling – he sure has a lot going on in his mind right now.

"You don't have to deny that the teleportation experiment was successful. I know it is. And I do not intend to get it from you forcefully – after all, it's your sweat. Rather, I want to buy it. With an invention like that, I will not suffer losses anymore in my business. My deliveries will be direct and prompt..." his face breaks off with a smile. "Don't think about it: I do not want to bore you with how important this invention of yours is to my business. And guess what? I am willing to pay huge money for it."

Garret thinks it is cowardice to continue to deny that he does not know what Ziko is talking about. Ziko is not acting on hearsay – from his words, Garret can tell that he is sure of what he is saying. He does not have a choice but to admit it.

"I am not selling my invention to anyone," he huffs – lines grow across his forehead. "By the way: how did you know that the experiment was successful? You're keeping tabs on me?"

"It doesn't matter how I found out. You (pointing the baton on Garret's chest) are going to sell the system to me. Sadly, you don't have a choice. But if you continue to refuse my offer..." he turns and goes back to his chair, adjusting his jacket, "then I will have no choice but to take it from you by force – and trust me, that would be tragic."

Garret giggles.

"Oh yeah, you like the sound of that, right?" Ziko joins in the giggle.

Garret soon breaks into laughter. The thugs holding him look amaze, wondering what is funny about what Ziko said.

"You really think you can threaten me?" Garret asks – the laughter has vanished from his face – his jaw squares.

"Oh no, it is not a threat. I don't threaten people. It just happens. After I say it, it becomes a part of your destiny. You can't help it."

"I see it was the reason you did all that to make sure I get the lab equipment..."

"Finally, someone understands my point!"

Garret sighs.

"Forget about it, Ziko. You are never going to get your hands on the system. Never!"

"Then I'm afraid I have to keep you here. You may be selling it out to the government. They will not appreciate it as much as I will…"

"The system is neither for you nor for the government. And keep me here all you want, but believe me, you will never get your hands on it."

Ziko's mouth stretches into a smile – this time, Garret wishes he could smack it off his face.

"The system is currently at Barnes' Laboratory. I can get it anytime I want. I only wanted to be as discreet as possible."

The surprise registers across Garret's face, but quickly fades away. This confirms once again that either there's a secret camera somewhere in the lab, or there's a mole amongst the employees.

"Since you have refused to agree to my proposal, then I have no choice but to obtain the system forcefully. And in doing that, I'm afraid things might get a little ugly."

Garret scrunches his face and tries to fight free from the men's grip, but they overpower him again, maintaining a tight grip. Ziko watches with a smile on his face.

"I like your tenacity, Garret, but give up. The system is mine once I get my hands on it." He turns to his boys. "Tie him to that chair over there (pointing) and come with me. We have some planning to make."

Garret pushes his feet backward on the ground with full resistance as the men drag him to the chair. The T-system is in the lab; he confirms in his mind. If Ziko gets his hands on it, he might not see it again. Now he's thinking of a way to contact Barny before the men raid the lab. But being tied to the chair, there isn't much he can do.

Meanwhile, Mr. Barnes is still in the lab that night. He sits in his office, with his phone in his hand. He scrolls through the call log and dials Garret's line. In fact, this is the umpteenth time he has dialed Garret's number. It hasn't been available. Mr. Barnes has left a number of voicemails and texts– one of which reads:

"Hey Garret, I don't know, but I have this strange feeling creeping up my guts – maybe it's because of what you told me about Agent Norman. I think we should move the T-system to a safer place. I don't know to where yet. Call me so we can discuss – or better still, come to the lab. I mean tonight."

But on the many voicemails and texts he's left, Garret has not replied. That's because he is not with his phone – one of Ziko's men has it. And now they've all gone to another part of the warehouse to make plans, just like Ziko said. If only he can convince the man with the phone to give it back.

Mr. Barnes stares absently at his phone. He is thinking of the best place to hide the T-system. He doesn't have to wait for Garret's permission. And the darker the night gets, the more dangerous it is for the T-system to remain in the laboratory.

Mr. Barnes looks around his office – the insecurity stares back at him. But his eyes settle on the crate that carries the T-system. A lot has been sacrificed already for him to watch the system get in the wrong hands. He takes a deep breath and gets on his feet. It is time to do something.

He dollies the crate towards the door. He looks around the office as if to make sure that he is not missing anything. He then switches off the light and shuts the door behind him.

15 minutes after Mr. Barnes left, a black jeep pulls over at the lab. Three of Ziko's men storm out – one of them had his nose broken by Garret. The injured spot has been bandaged, and now he's ready for more action.

The lights give them a clear view of the surroundings as they take a survey. At a glance, it may seem like they are not armed – but they have their guns tucked down their waists.

One of them looks at the other two and gives a nod toward the lab. Having not drawn their guns tells that they are certain of the level of security around the lab. They probably know that they will not find anyone in the lab.

Gaining entrance, they will have to break through the steel door. It clangs as they push it vigorously. One of them finally pulls out his gun and points it at the door.

"Not here, Josh," the other thug cautions. "The roof." He looks up.

Josh shoves his gun back down his waist and looks up. His eyes fall on a window across the front wall. It has an extended windowsill from which they can get their hands on the roof.

"There!" he points.

He goes over to the window. It seems like that of Mr. Barnes' office. But it has protective steel bars. If they have to go through the window, then it will be a lot of work pulling out the security bars. The roof is there best plan to enter the building.

Josh places his hand on the lower windowsill and leaps to the upper one. He pushes himself up, with his feet now on the lower windowsill. He supports his stance by grabbing a steel pipe jutting out from the wall. From the top windowsill, he leaps again. His hands land expertly on the roof. Had he not applied enough momentum before leaping, he would have landed back on the ground, and perhaps smashing his jaw against the lower windowsill.

Now settled on the asphalt surface of the flat roof, he walks around for an easier spot to break through. As there is no access to the inside except for the large skylights. The second man soon joins him on the roof – not too long, the last man follows.

Right above Garret's department is one of the skylights. With a hard hit using the butt of their gun, the glass of the skylight breaks. Splinters of glass rain down. Josh and the other thugs jump down thru the broken skylight, landing on one of the lab tables.

They get on their feet and begin to search the whole lab. Having thoroughly ransacked Garret's department, they move over to other parts of the lab. They find their way to the Clean Room, the central unit and even to Mr. Barnes' office – everywhere.

"I can't find it, I think someone moved it," Josh concedes, letting off some air through his nostrils.

"Yeah, I think so too," the other men agree.

They look around one more time and then the last man urges them:

"Let's get outta here, before the police show up…"

CHAPTER NINE:
BAD GUYS

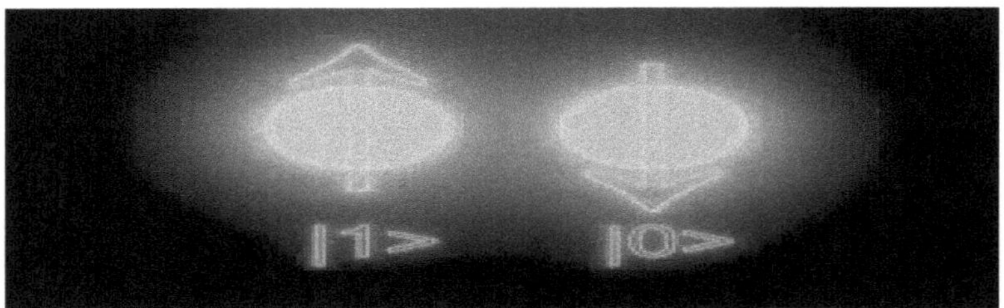

"You asked to see me, sir," Agent Norman answers.

He is standing in the Director's office, with his hands behind and a devoted look on his face. The Director is standing by the window, with his fingers on the blinds. The streaks of grey in his hair suggest he's gone past his 50s. His black suit camouflages with the color of the chair beside him.

"Garret Strong was supposed to be here this morning. What is going on?" the Director asks, still looking out the window – a hand in his pocket.

"I don't know, sir. I might have to put a call across his line…"

"Or better still go to his house."

"Yes sir."

The Director finally drops his fingers from the blind and turns to Agent Norman. His bulbous nose sits on a face with thin wrinkles. He turns the chair and drops his bottom on it, swiveling lightly from left to right – all eyes on Agent Norman.

"I don't have to tell you how great his invention is," he continues. "I don't have to tell you that if it gets into the wrong hands, we would be at the mercy of some evil tyrants like the Chinese or the Russians. We must get him to sell the system to us no matter what."

"I understand perfectly, sir. He's pretty stubborn – but I'll find a way to convince him."

"Do whatever you can and bring him to my office. Am I clear on that?"

"Perfectly, sir."

The Director waves his hands and looks down at the file on the table. Agent Norman turns toward the door. But then, a knock comes through.

"Come in," the Director looks up.

An agent walks into the office, adjusting his glasses.

"I'm sorry, sir, but we think Garret has been kidnapped," he reports.

Agent Norman stops in his tracks and looks back.

"Kidnapped? By whom?" the Director questions – his nose flares.

"We think it's by the Sinaloa Drug Cartel. We saw the footage of the kidnap along his street."

The Director's eyes and those of Agent Norman meet. The message is pretty clear to Norman why the Director glanced at him.

"If you would like to see the street-cam footage, sir," the other agent adds.

The Director stands on his feet and gestures toward the door. The two agents make their way through the door – the Director follows.

The second agent leads the way through a narrow corridor. He veers to the right, through a door that leads into the spacious control room. There are other agents here, and a line of computers screens.

The agent goes over to one of the computers and sets his hands on the mouse. Agent Norman and the Director watch as he clicks from one thumbnail to another. Agent Norman fears what will happen if the Cartel get their hands on the system. It will be just like the Director said.

The footage comes on screen. It shows the moment Garret comes to light, and begins to look around. And after a while, it shows a huge man charge in from behind and smashes his head with a baton. Still in the footage, Garret is carried away, into the dark – just beyond the area the security camera covers.

"How did you know it's the Sinaloa Drug Cartel?" the Director inquires.

The agent places his hand on the mouse again and takes the footage back to where the attacker charged in. He clicks pause and then zooms in on his head. There's a small circle with an 'X' at the center at the back of his head. The Director's face turns pale – his eyes unblinking. Quite notably, he recognizes this tattoo.

"Unfortunately, there's nothing in the video that can tell us to where Garret has been taken," Agent Norman quips.

"I'll have to make some phone calls." The Director walks out of the control room.

Agent Norman stares vacantly at the screen for a while before heading out the door too.

***

Ziko storms to where Garret is sitting and gives him an eye-reeling slap. Garret's face is thrown to the side. The men have returned and have given their reports. Ziko barely hides his fury and disappointment behind a smile, even after he slapped Garret.

"You smart American fool! Where have you taken the system?"

Garret raises his face. A smile breaks the corners of his mouth apart.

"Look who's been all about not getting upset. Now he calls me a smart fool…"

He swallows a lump of saliva and giggles. The smile on Ziko's face has cleared this time. His eyes are burning with the rage he tries to conceal.

"You still haven't answered my question: where have you taken the system?" he flares.

"I don't know what you're talking about…"

"Don't give me that crap! You know what I'm talking about."

Garret is quiet for a moment. He glances at the men standing around him, waiting for the order to pounce on him. But whatever they plan to do to him, he is glad that they did not find the T-system. He is once again grateful to Mr. Barnes whom he thinks must have changed the location.

"Somehow, you knew that the T-system is at Barnes' laboratory. You've had me tied up here the whole night. You have my phone. How the hell do you think I would have called for the relocation of the system?"

"I don't care. You may not have called for it, but you sure know where it's been taken…"

"I don't!"

Ziko draws in a deep breath, with his eyes shut. He exhales, glaring at Garret.

"I told you before: it's a different world out here. It's my jungle, and I am the king. I can drill the information out of you. I can do the worst things to you, Garret Strong. So, I'm gonna ask again: where is the system?"

"You are desperate, Ziko. It's obvious. Even your men here, if they are not as desperate as you are, knows that it's pointless you continuing to ask me this question. I do not know where it is…"

Ziko fires a punch to his face and then grabs his neck.

"You think I'm here for jokes, huh? Yes, I'm desperate – if that's what you wanna hear." He tightens his grip around Garret's neck. "Where is it? Where is the system? Where did you hide it?" He squeezes tighter, shaking Garret's head. "You wanna play hard, huh? Is that it?"

"That's enough, Ziko," a voice orders from behind with a heavy Spanish accent.

Ziko recognize the voice at once. He stops and slowly withdraws his hands from Garret. The color in his eye starts to fade. Garret's chest rises and falls rapidly as he gulps down fresh air and swallows hard.

As Garret withdraws from Ziko, the man from behind replaces him. He is tall and wearing a black suit. His presence is preceded by the authority he commands. His round face is half covered with grey beard – even his eye brows are grey. He's got small almond eyes like buttons – they give a cold gaze synonymous to that of a killer. But at this moment, he squints as he lets off a cloud of smoke from his mouth. His face crinkles as his fingers hold a thin cigar. His imposing personality quickly grips the men – those of them that have been sitting are forced to get on their feet. Garret can tell that he is their boss, El Jefe. In Spanish the term means 'King or Boss' mostly applied when referring to cartel leaders.

"I have told you, Ziko: always try to control your temper," his voice is of a perfect Spanish baritone – it squeezes the air around it tightly as it travels.

Now he turns to Garret, with the thin cigar in his mouth. He stares at him as though it's his first time seeing a human before – or perhaps he's amazed at how much he's been battered already by Ziko and his men.

"I want to trust you, Mr. Garret. I have a feeling we can be partners for a long time. Soooo…"

He stands back. Behind a cloud of smoke, he looks at one of the thugs and gestures his head at Garret. The man moves in and begins to untie Garret. The boss watches, puffing grey clouds into the air. Ziko's rage appears to have subsided – his facial color has returned. He just stands and gazes at Garret, with his hand across his upper jaw.

Garret has been untied. He stretches his arms and massages the point bruised by the ropes. It dawns on him once again the significance of freedom. He wipes his mouth with his shirt and gets on his feet, wincing.

"My apologies for the way my boys have treated you," the boss intones. "Ziko has anger management issues – the reason he always hides behind a smile."

"What do you want?" Garret asks, massaging his wrists.

He knows the boss' kindness is not for nothing. And he is starting to understand the kind of business Ziko has been talking about.

"I do not think it is wise we discuss that now. You don't look good enough. Why don't you come with me? Let's get you cleaned up."

Garret wants to turn down this offer. Of course he already knows what the boss wants. He's just approaching it in a way different from that of Ziko's. But whatever way it is, Garret will not fall for it. However, the eyes that glare back at him when he looked around forced him to submit for now.

"All right…?" he agrees.

"Please pardon me. You can call me Senior Ramirez."

Garret nods lightly.

"This way, please," Sr. Ramirez gestures toward the exit.

As Garret walks by his side, he glances at the men around him. There's complete distrust in their eyes that he will continue to be loyal. And so the group of thugs are looking for his next move. They know he will try to run – and truly, that has been the only thought in his mind since he was untied. He's been hoping that the men will let their guard down for a moment, and he will take off. But he also knows that one wrong move could earn him a bullet in the head.

***

Meanwhile, Mr. Barnes is talking with a police officer at the lab. Earlier today, he's been to Garret's house to check on him. There's a deep feeling inside of him that something has happened to Garret. And so, he has not only reported the destruction in the lab to the police, but Garret's possible kidnap as well.

"I honestly do not know who could have done this – but I hope you find them soon," he tells the officer.

"Did you have a misunderstanding with anyone – you know, something that could lead to this (pointing at the destruction in the skylight)?" the officer interrogates.

"Not at all," Mr. Barnes replies. "I've been working on equipment and experiments in my lab, alongside the young man I told you about.

We have always done our best to deliver promptly to our customers – no problems at all."

Mr. Barnes does not want to tell him about the T-system. He does not want to tell him that it's probably the reason Garret was kidnapped. He thinks he will be worsening the situation if he tells the officer about it.

The officer turns to the building briefly, and then back at Mr. Barnes.

"This looks to me like whoever it is was looking for something. Do you have anything that might have attracted them – maybe a piece of equipment or something?"

"Except the person has knowledge for quantum physics, if not, then there's nothing special in the lab. There are just pieces of laboratory equipment."

"And the young man that you believe has been kidnapped…"

"His name is Garret Strong."

"Yeah, Garret – was he in conflict with anyone – anyone at all that might have instigated his kidnap?"

"No. He was all about his project."

"That project of his, do you think he was working with his own formula, or maybe he stole it from another scientist?"

"My boy is unique – his formulas are unique as well. He works them out himself."

The officer's shoulders drop. Interrogating Mr. Barnes is not leading him anywhere in his investigation, he thinks. There's definitely more to the whole story than mere breaking and entering and kidnapping.

"I'll have to question your employees as well," he tells Mr. Barnes.

"Of course, go ahead…"

***

In the eastern part of the city, Garret is being driven in a black Chevy Suburban to Sr. Ramirez's house. He has nothing binding his hands and legs. Sr. Ramirez is convinced he can strike a partnership with him. He believes he will be much easier to convince if he has his freedom. But Garret thinks that is a mistake on his own part.

As they drive along the road, Garret has been looking for a means to escape. His eyes have been everywhere, hoping for a chance. But he can't jump out of the Suburban while it's speeding along the freeway. He is hoping that there's stopover somewhere. Although Sr. Ramirez sits next to the door, Garret believes he can knock him out with ease when it's time to escape. Sr. Ramirez has been making efforts to raise an engaging conversation between them, but Garret's one-word replies frustrate his motive.

"Pull over in front of the building by the right, Jason. I want to get a nice bottle of wine," Sr. Ramirez orders.

And finally, the opportunity Garret has been waiting for has arrived. There are three other men in the Suburban. The driver is one of the three. There is also a big thug sitting in the front passenger seat and one other thug sitting in the back next to Garret, they are all armed. There's also a van behind the Suburban – it is where Ziko and the other men are. Garret has to be fast enough to elude them.

The Suburban comes to a halt in front of a fine wine store. Sr. Ramirez adjusts his coat.

"I hope you like red wine. Oh, you don't stand a chance if you try to escape," he tells Garret. "Stay here to avoid getting hurt." He taps Garret's thigh and opens the side door to exit.

126

Once Sr. Ramirez steps out of the door Garret could make his escape. Garret thought of using Sr. Ramirez as a leverage, but the surroundings are too open. Something might go wrong.

Sr. Ramirez swaggers out of the Suburban and pulls on his coat. The door starts to shut. Garret is about to storm out of the van, but one of the men comes and takes over Sr. Ramirez's position. Garret is not deterred, nonetheless. He merely glances at the thug, while building up momentum in his muscles.

The door is closing and about to shut. It is time!

Garret elbows the neck of the man that had taken over Sr. Ramirez's position and dashes out of the Suburban. He sprints along the sidewalk and veers off through an alley. Ziko and his men respond immediately. They storm out of the van and give Garret a chase – their guns are drawn. The men in the van had to process what just happen giving Garret an opportunity to flee.

Garret zips across the road, vaulting over cars and bollards. He has no idea where he is headed at this point. He just wants to get as far away from the men as possible. Ziko is the first to fire a shot in his path. Garret ducks. The bullet tears through the wall of a building nearby. Screams erupt everywhere. People start to scamper for safety.

Garret jumps over a short steel fence surrounding a city park. Bullets tear into the ground as he runs haphazardly across the grass. Ziko and his men continue to trail behind. With his attempt to escape, Garret sure knows that he has angered Sr. Ramirez. But at this point, it didn't matter.

As he whips past a statue, it is hit by a bullet. He ducks and goes behind a fountain, from whence he runs through a narrow path. He is almost crushed by a car as he dashes out onto the street. But his reflexes reacted on time. He leaps across the car – his hands giving the support.

Now he finds himself in a two-lane road. Landing on his feet, he is faced with a bus driving right at him. Cars toot their horns rather ceremoniously as he avoids getting run over by the city bus. Garret makes his way across the street. He glanced backwards and noticed that Ziko and his men are still coming. Cars are honking their horns, trying not to run over any of the men-pursuing Garret.

Garret finally makes it out of the road, through an alleyway. But upon reaching the exit, two of Ziko's men storm out, blocking him off. He wants to run backwards, but one of them has his gun leveled at him. The other man is the one that got an elbow to the neck. His bloodshot eyes read that he has a score to settle with Garret. He does not have a gun – just physical combat, he believes.

Garret has his hands in the air as the men march closer. It will be the end of him if the others come here. If only he can make it through this alleyway, he believes the men will no longer find him.

"So much for running, huh?" the man with the gun boasts!

He stands about a yard away from Garret. The other man leers, rubbing his hands together.

"You piss me off so bad I wish I could just end you right here and right now. But the boss wants you alive, and perhaps unharmed. So I want you to put your hands behind your head and turn around slowly."

Garret hesitates

"NOW!"

Garret slowly raises his hands to the back of his head, shifting his eyes between the men and the gun. He turns around, still looking over his shoulders.

"Get him."

The man Garret elbowed moves in. But as he tries to grab Garret's hands, Garret turns sharply and grabs his hand instead, pulling him into his grip. Now he has his arm tight around the thug's neck, a classic rear choke hold. It all happened so fast the guy with the gun didn't see it coming. But Garret does not have a weapon. He rather wants to use this man as a leverage to escape or as a cover if the other villain decides to shoot.

"Let him go," the thug orders.

"Drop your gun," Garret blares.

"I said, let him go!"

"Calm down, man – don't shoot," the man held by Garret begs between stifled breaths.

But the look in his fellow's eyes already suggests he's about to pull the trigger. Garret can see his finger moving through micro distances to the trigger.

"Drop the gun…" he barks.

But the man pulls the trigger. Fortunately, the gun goes click not bang. He hadn't noticed that he used up all his bullets while chasing Garret. Now Garret has to fight his way through.

The man hurls his 38 pistol at Garret, but it hits his man in the face instead. He yells. Garret tightens the grip on him, while keeping his eyes on the other man.

The thug in Garret's hold tries to fight free. He sends an elbow backward, but Garret shifts to the other side. And that gives the thug the opportunity to force his body to the side. As he struggles to the remove Garret's arms around his neck, the other man plunges himself at Garret, knocking him to the ground. The other man finally regains his freedom.

The thug storms to where Garret is. He tries to pull him up. But Garret quickly gets on his feet, lifts him off the ground and throws him overhead. His back lands squarely on the bare ground. As the other man moves in, Garret sends a kick to his face. He drops to the ground and does not get up again.

Garret looks back. Ziko and his men are coming from the other way. He bolts. They fire several gunshots in his path, but he continues to run. Before he makes it out of the alleyway, he hears one of the thugs yell after a gunshot. He must have been hit. That's to Garret's advantage - one man down.

From the alleyway, he runs toward the left, panting for breath. Ziko and the men are trying to keep up. They may be firing shots in his path, but they would prefer to catch him alive. If they will kill him after they've extracted the information they need, it will be slow and painful - a way of punishing him for putting them through this stress. That is if they get their hands on Garret. But he's not going to let that happen.

Right ahead is a crowded sidewalk. It's like a procession of crazy shoppers. There's no way the men will fire gunshots here. Garret runs quickly and disappears within the crowd.

Ziko and his men soon arrive at the scene, breathing heavily, with their guns in their hands.

"We have to spread out to cover more grounds," Ziko yells between breaths. "There are too many people here. He hasn't gone far. He must be among these people."

The men are exhausted - the wrinkles on their faces can tell. Ziko leads the way - they have no choice but to follow.

Meanwhile, Garret has wound his way out of the crowd. Now he's along the road, skipping as fast as he can and looking back.

Suddenly, he is grabbed and pulled out of the road into a women's boutique shop. He fights free at once and sends a punch toward the face of whoever grabbed him. His massive fist is just a few inches away from impact when he recognizes whom it is.

"Judy?" he calls - his face rumples with surprise. "What are you doing here?" he questions.

She is dressed in a thick leather jacket and trouser. A baseball cap hides her hair made in a ponytail. Her feet sheltered in a pair of black boots all give her that bad-girl feeling.

"I saw some guys running after you. It was hard to keep up. But then I was standing somewhere in the crowd when I saw you mix with them. Somehow, I just knew you would come through this path so I waited here."

Garret is still trying to catch his breath. The contractions in his muscles are yet to settle. He'll be off at the sight of the men.

"I have to get out of here. Can you find a way to talk to Barny?" he intones.

"Barny?" Judy's face crumples.

"Yeah, Mr. Barnes…"

"Oh… but who are those guys? What do they want from you?"

"It's a long story, Judy. Maybe we should talk about it later. I have to get to my house." Garret glances at the road.

"Your house? Don't you think they would be waiting for you there?"

Garret looks at Judy. Smart thinking!

"I think you're right. Then I have to go to Barny's for now. Sorry, Judy, but I have to go."

Immediately Garret takes a step out of the shop, he sees the men stomping along the road. At the same time, Judy pulls him back and covers the side of his face with her head – the other hand on his neck as though she's in a hot romance with her boyfriend. She takes

Garret's hand and places it on her waist, and then her leg wraps around that of Garret's – all that to create as much cover as possible. Ziko and his men glance into the shop as they run past it – but neither of them notices that Garret is in there.

"They've gone," she reports.

Garret looks at the road briefly and then back at Judy. They both stare into each other's eyes like in the movies. That moment of cover has created a spark between them. For a moment, Garret forgets the trouble he is in and stares at the twinkles in Judy's eyes. There's a movement of their heads toward each other.

But then, Garret breaks out, having realized quickly what is about to happen.

"I – I have to go now. Thank you."

He turns to leave, but Judy pulls him back again.

"No, Garret – even Mr. Barnes' house isn't safe for you. You'll only put him in greater danger if you go to his house…"

"Greater danger? What do you mean?"

"The lab was broken into last night. According to the police, whomever it is appeared to be searching for something. It's obvious anyway, seeing how they turned the whole place upside down, even damaging some equipment. I think it's these men that are after you. Seeing how close you are to Mr. Barnes, I believe they will also have their eyes on him. So I advise you don't go around him for now."

Garret turns back, running his hand across his hair and then settling it on his jaw. He fears he may have put Mr. Barnes' life at risk – even his small laboratory is under attack.

"You can use my apartment, if you don't mind," Judy offers.

Wrinkles grow across Garret's face. He is not sure what she means.

"Your place?" he questions.

"For now, yes," she answers almost in a whisper.

"Sorry, I can't Judy…"

"Yes, you can. You need to go to somewhere they will not find you. Maybe you'll make plans on how to handle the problem while you're there. Your house is no longer safe, neither is Mr. Barnes' – not even the laboratory is safe – nowhere else is safe for you right now, Garret."

Garret may be reluctant to accept the offer, but he knows there's sense in what she's saying. He has spent all his money purchasing the necessary lab equipment. He doesn't have much of a choice at the moment.

"All right…" he agrees.

"Good. Come with me." Judy cuts in so quick that it seems he will change his mind a second after.

"But I need to talk to Barny first. It's important."

"You will talk to him when we get to my place. It's risky being out here. Let's go…"

Judy drags him along as they try to stay undetected while walking down road looking for a taxi. Garret is considering in his mind about telling Judy what exactly is going on. She's also putting herself into danger by allowing him stay with her. With that, he thinks she deserves to know about everything.

CHAPTER TEN: GARRET'S SURPRISE

Garret could not retrieve his phone from Ziko and his men. But with Judy's phone, he was able to reach Mr. Barnes. They were to meet at the park somewhere at the heart of the city.

Mr. Barnes has been waiting for Garret in the grassy area of the park. There was relief in his heart when Garret called him the first time. He probably thought he would be facing serious drilling at the hands of Ziko and his men.

He soon spots Garret coming toward him. That relief he felt the first time is complete now. But even with the apparent air of complacency, caution must not be thrown to the wind. They will both have to keep their eyes out for Ziko.

"Good to see you again, son," Barny comments, shaking hands with Garret. "Those guys must have done you bad," he observes the slight bruises and swellings on Garret's face.

"Not really - they were just trying to get their way," Garret replies, glancing over his shoulders. "Heard the lab was invaded," he adds.

"Yeah. But nothing I can't handle. I'm just worried about you."

"You don't have to. I'll be fine. I'm just thinking maybe you should stay away from the lab for now."

"You're kidding, right?" Barny chuckles.

"I'm not. Those guys are desperate. And they won't hesitate to remove anyone that stands in their way."

Barny is staring toward the far end of the field - the corners of his eyes crinkling.

"I can't run away from my laboratory because some hooligans want something I can't give..."

"It's not running away, Barny," Garret cuts in. "Being linked to me, I fear your life is in danger."

"You should be more worried about yourself, son. I'll be ready for them if they return."

Garret surrenders with a deep breath. He knows there's no way Barny will agree to abandon his laboratory. But that seems to be the best idea, nonetheless.

"What about the T-system and my laptop?" Garret inquires.

"They're locked up, down in the basement at the old farm house. It's the safest place I can think of."

Garret nods.

"Good. It stays there until the dust settles," Barny adds.

Garret scans their surroundings. It's all peaceful. The children are playing around, with their parents keeping watchful eyes on them.

"What about the CIA? I think you should go and see the director. They'll offer you protection..."

"In exchange for the T-system," Garret interrupts. "No, I don't need their protection."

"But you can't keep ignoring their invitation. You have to go and find out what they want. They might make you a good offer you know."

"I don't..."

"Talk to them first, son."

Garret's shoulders drop. He sighs. Mr. Barnes' words registers in his mind. It's indeed wise that he hears them out first.

"I'll go to the office tomorrow," he finally agrees.

"Great. That's a step in the right direction."

"And then one more thing: I think I've got an idea on how we can get these guys out of our backs for now."

"What idea is that?" Barny looks at Garret briefly and then returns his eyes to the distance.

"What if we build another T-system, with one or two of the equipment missing? And even if it's complete, they will not have the formula to actually make it work. What do you think?"

"It's not really about the T-system, Garret. It's about the formula you created. The T-system does not contain any new or special piece of equipment. The primary focus is the computer formula that operates it to teleport objects. And that is why they are after you."

Garret gives a second thought to his idea. It sounds to him as though he's desperate to get the cartel off his back. And Garret deciphers that maybe it's because it is him the cartel wants, that's why Barny doesn't want to stay away from the laboratory. However, it is an eye-opener as to the depth of trouble he's in.

He surveys his surroundings again and reclines on the bench.

"I reported the breaking and entering and your kidnap to the police," Barny breaks the silence between them. "Although I didn't tell them the possible reason the lab was broken into, and the people believed to have kidnapped you. They will have to figure that out themselves."

"Even if they figure it out, I think it'll take a lot more to get the cartel off my back."

"We can't be sure about that."

Another silence lingers between them. But it is broken again by Barny.

"At Judy's, right?"

"Yeah," Garret answers.

Barny exhales. "Nowhere is entirely safe for now. So always be on the lookout...Stay frosty!"

"Always..."

"Although I would have asked that you come live with me. We can both face them squarely when they come - but I know you wouldn't agree to that."

"No, I wouldn't. I don't want you to get involved more than you already have."

There's no point stressing it - Barny gives up.

"Please stay on the lookout always, and don't work too late in the lab," Garret advices.

"I've seen way too much to be afraid of those boys. I'll be ready for them, if they come."

It's impossible to convince Barny of the danger ahead. Garret wonders how he will fight off about 10 men alone. He fears for

Barny's life. But Barny seems absolutely unperturbed. Rather, he's ready for battle.

"The question now is: how do we stop these men from coming after us?" Garret asks.

Barny interlocks his fingers around his groin area, still looking far into the field.

"For now, I don't know. Until the police complete their investigation and wade fully into the case, we just have to continue to protect ourselves from them..."

Garret purses his lips and shrugs.

"Or maybe after you've talked with the CIA, they will take it up against the cartel," Barny chips in.

"Whatever help the CIA offers, it'll come at a cost – and we both know what it is. That's not how I want it to be..."

It is for the sake of respect for Barny, and perhaps for the government that Garret agreed to honor the director's invitation. He already knows the topic to be discussed. And no matter what their offer is, he will not sell out his invention. He has worked so hard to have his name written in the history books. Selling the ownership of the T-system removes his name from those books. He's not ready to trade that recognition for anything.

Garret and Mr. Barnes leave the Park through different routes.

"We should not be seen together. It's not safe," Garret told Barny.

Barny does not really agree with that, but for Garret's sake, he acts accordingly.

Garret is out of the Park. With his hands in his jacket, he marches along the walkway for a taxi. His searching eyes pierce through every corner. That usual feeling is up his guts again - someone is following him.

He waves his hand at a taxi, but it does continue on its way. Standing at a spot isn't safe, Garret thinks. He walks on, waving his hand at different taxis, but none seems to be going his way.

There's a road on the other side - maybe he will get a taxi there.

He walks through a narrow alleyway and out to the road.

A moment after he walks through the alleyway, a gunshot is fired. He does not bother to check if the shot was at him or not, he quickly withdraws into the alley. He can hear the screams of people. It appears someone has been hit.

Garret does not run through the alleyway, he crouches by the wall of a building, peeping out to the road.

From here, he sees a man storming toward the entrance to the alley. He is tall and brawny. His brown Asian skin blends with his black shirt and black trouser. And like death in the night, his long black coat flaps in the wind. His black boots show no pity as they stomp the ground. With his hands hidden in black gloves, his intent seems clear. His eyes are hidden behind dark sunshades - typical of an assassin. His imposing personality gives shivers down the spines of bystanders as he marches along. Garret has not seen him before. And it is obvious the shot came from his gun. Maybe Sr. Ramirez got so angry and sent his worst assassin at him, Garret thinks.

Garret remains in position, watching as the man bounces closer. He wants to be sure the man is after him, at the same time, ready for a showdown.

The man has his gun leveled at Garret at the sight of him. Garret raises his hands and steps deeper into the alley.

"Who are you? What do you want?" Garret asks.

The man stares at Garret through the sunshade, not saying a word. His hand is steady on the gun - his index just leaning on the trigger.

"My boss wants to talk to you," he croaks. With a Chinese accent.

"And who is your boss?" Garret has his feet solid on the ground - not a bit of nervousness in his voice.

The man is silent again for a while. Since Garret cannot see his eyes, he is focused on the movement of his index around the trigger.

"There's a car parked down the road," the man speaks. "You will walk calmly to it. You will get the answers to your questions."

"And what if I refuse to follow you?"

Garret notices the corner of the man's mouth goes up slightly. He fires a shot on the ground, next to where Garret is standing. Big mistake!

In three fluid movements, Garret jumps out of harm's way, glides across the ground and grabs the man's hand as he tries to shoot at him. A scuffle breaks out between them. The man seems stronger than Garret. He tries to bend the gun toward Garret's belly. But Garret puts in equal resistance, forcing the gun toward the man's belly instead.

But then, the man, with his left hand, smites Garret's neck. His intent could have been to knock Garret out, but he only crashes to the ground, releasing his hold on the gun. But as the man tries to reposition himself over Garret, a kick sends the gun flying off his hand and clattering on the ground some distance away.

Garret scrambles to his feet immediately - his hands balled into fists.

The man walks from left to right - his bulky frame seems to have grown twice what it was. Ready for physical combat, he does not remove his sunshades - not even a twitch of the muscles. He is confident he will take Garret down with one punch.

He stomps forward in a martial arts stance. Garret sends a blow from the right - he dodges it - from the left, he dodges it. Another shot toward his lower jaw, he catches Garret's fist - and with immense strength, he hurls Garret across the air. His back slams against the wall and he thuds to the ground.

The man charges in again and drags Garret off the ground. But as Garret's legs leave the ground, he pushes them forward. They jam against the man's legs, knocking them off the ground. His huge body bounces on the ground.

With all his extensive martial arts training, his assailant knows it is taboo to be in this position, he gets back on his feet - his glasses still in position. He charges forward, but Garret has regained his balance at this time.

Garret dodges his punches and kicks. He tries to grab Garret by the neck, but Garret holds his hand in a vice-like grip. However, that earns Garret a head-butt. Garret falls backward.

Even before Garret regains his balance this time, the man swoops in and removes him from the ground. He lifts his whole body in the air and slams it on the ground, WWE style. Garret lets out a grunt.

Now the man gets on top of Garret and begins to fire punches to his face. Garret blocks off as many as he can, while some penetrate the wall over his face.

Garret with a buck of his hips and a hard roll to his right forces the man off of him. Garret staggers back on his feet.

The man charges forward again, going for another slam. Garret leaps in the air and delivers a jaw-breaking kick with his knee to his face. The man falls four steps backward. The impact keeps him disoriented for a moment. He probably wasn't expecting it. Garret sees to a vulnerable opportunity that his assailant has exposed.

He fires punches to the man's ribs and face - and then a powerful kick to the middle of his face. He falls back but not on the ground. Garret runs, leaps and smashes his jaw with another punch. Still, his feet remain on the ground.

Now Garret swoops in and lifts his whole weight off the ground. With the man up in the air, Garret takes two steps backward and slams him hard on the ground - his glasses fly off of his face, revealing a pair or beady, asian eyes.

Garret waddles, breathing hard. He staggers to where the gun is and picks it up. He comes back and stands over the man.

"I'm not a killer," he affirms.

Expertly, he disassembles the gun. He takes out the magazine and flings the gun back to where he picked it.

"Now you tell your boss, whoever it is, that I am not interested in whatever he wants to say. Get off my back!"

The man is still on the ground as Garret walks out of the alleyway, with victory right across his shoulders and head held high.

However, it dawns on Garret that the Sinaloa Drug Cartel is not the only group after him. With this man, it is clear some Chinese group – maybe an Asian drug organization or the Chinese government are after him as well.

There is no way he can let any criminal organization or foreign government have access or take control of the T-system. If he gets captured he might not return alive. They will do all sorts of things to wangle out information from him. Maybe talking with the CIA will have some men watch his back.

***

Garret arrives at Judy's place – an apartment in the southern part of DC. Judy lives in a two-bedroom room loft on the top floor. As safe as this place may seem, Garret is still cautious of the surroundings. He trudges up the staircase, looking over his shoulders.

As he gets to the door, he hears Judy humming in the living room. It seems like she is talking to someone on the phone. Garret stops and leans his ear lightly against the door. But the humming soon fades away, as if she knows that someone is at the door.

Garret sighs and reluctantly knocks on the door. In his situation, he feels he must not trust anyone, except Barny. But Judy has proven to be trustworthy. Maybe he is just allowing his distrust of people cloud his sense of reasoning, he thinks.

Judy opens the door. "Oh my goodness! What happened to you," Judy sparks upon seeing how beat-up Garret looks.

She leads him to the couch. Garret lets out a loud breath as he settles in on the comfortable couch.

"What happened to you?" Judy rephrases, sitting on the arm of the couch.

"Met a man on my way back," Garret narrates. "He says his boss wants to talk to me. I refused and we started dancing."

"A man? Who is he? Did he mention who his boss is?" Judy's face creases lightly.

"He didn't. But I think he's from a different cartel or foreign government. He had a very heavy Chinese accent..."

"Oh yeah, we should have seen that coming..." Judy goes and settles in a small chair opposite that of Garret's.

"How do you mean?" Garret inquires.

"The Asian cartel are heavily involved in drug trafficking - and with an invention like yours, they can teleport drugs around the world.

They have their noses almost everywhere. They must have sniffed out the details of your invention."

"We can't be so sure that they are drug traffickers."

"Trust me they are."

Garret scratches his chin.

"You seem to know a lot about these people..."

Judy reclines on the couch.

"My brother was a drug dealer. He got too deep in the cartel and that cost him his life."

Garret heaves a sigh. It is not right that he doesn't trust Judy as much as he should - and his conscience beats him for that.

"Why don't you go and take a shower? I'll make you something to eat," Judy intones.

"Yeah... That sounds great, I'm really hungry"

Garret only hopes that these running and attacks stop soon. It may seem like he doesn't know what to do - how to stop the men. He has not forgotten his trainings from the Navy Seal programs. He can reach out to his friends for help. But he thinks the T-system must not come to light on the basis of bloodshed. He hopes that everything will resolve itself soon.

However, it seems like the more he hopes the worse things get. With the attack today, he fears more like it will come. Maybe it's time to handle it the military way - maybe it's time to activate the dark side of Garret Strong.

***

The next day, Garret is in the director's office. He sits in the chair opposite that of the director's, glancing at almost everything in the office. In his mind is a resolve that no matter what, he will not sell the ownership of the T-system to the government. The director has just left to attend to an issue in the control room. Agent Norman is not in the building at this time. Maybe he would be sitting in the chair next to Garret.

"My apologies for keeping you waiting, Mr. Strong," the Director intones, walking through the door.

He comes and settles himself in the chair, reclined.

"Through our surveillance camera, we discovered that you were kidnapped by men of the Sinaloa Drug Cartel," he explains. "We couldn't round up for a rescue because there was no way we could find out to where you were taken. Agents Norman and Stephanie are still investigating the kidnap. However, I'm glad you're here now. You see..."

He gets up from the chair and shoves his hands in his pocket, walking toward the window.

"You've already made a name for yourself. But we want to announce it to the whole world. We want to present your invention on a global stage. The invention remains in your name. All we want..." He comes and leans against the edge of his table, next to Garret. "...is to make sure this invention of yours does not get into the wrong hands. I'm pretty sure you know why you were kidnapped by the cartel. The CIA will help you fight them off. And your name will be written on a gold plaque."

Now he goes back to his chair and sits down - Garret's eyes meets with his. If he is not in denial, he will see the resolve on Garret's face. He doesn't appear broken even after all the Director has explained.

"We want you to sell the ownership of the system to us. But we will maintain your name as the original inventor. This is to make sure it does not get into the wrong hands, like I said before. If it does, we will have a lot of illegal drugs smuggled into this country, right under our noses. Undetectable! I need you to give this a serious thought."

Garret clears his throat - confidence in his eyes and on his lips.

"I'm sorry, sir, but I do not want to sell the ownership of the system. And you can be rest assured that it will not get into the wrong hands."

The Director knocks his pen rhythmically on the table - eyes fixed on Garret as if he can see his thoughts.

"There must be a reason why you don't want to sell the ownership of the system to the government, right?" he interrogates.

"Not exactly. Besides, I'm still working on it."

"Well, we can build you one of the best research laboratories in the country to complete your project."

"Thanks for the offer, sir, but I'd rather stay at Barnes' Laboratory."

"Isn't it too small for such a huge project?"

"It has all I need."

The Director exhales, knocks the pen on the table and reclines on the chair. He seems to have given up.

"What about the Sinaloa Drug Cartel – how do you get them off your back? Surely you're not gonna sign some agreement with them or something."

"I'll take care of that, sir."

"And how do you intend to do that?"

"Let me worry about that."

The Director tries to keep his expression plain, but Garret notices his face turning crimson, and his lips tightening. The discussion is not leading anywhere and it's starting to infuriate him, even though he tries to hide it.

"Well, Mr. Strong..." he pushes closer and rests his arms on the desk. "I will advise you give our proposal a second thought. Your invention is safest with the U.S. government, and you know that. But if you maintain the right to it and it gets into the wrong hands and is being used to initiate crimes, or a matter of National security, then I'm afraid you will also go in for it..."

"With all due respect, sir, I think this last statement is coming from you. I think you're taking this too personal..."

"What do you mean?" The Director has totally gone red in the face as his anger becomes more obvious.

"Do you arrest the inventor of a rifle because it was used by someone else to kill the president?"

"Well..." The Director's eyelids flutter.

"If we are done here, sir, I beg to take my leave."

The Director reclines on his chair, glaring at Garret, twiddling his thumbs.

"You may go," he gestures with his right arm.

"Thank you, sir."

Garret gets on his feet and heads straight to the door.

"Mr. Strong!" the Director calls.

Garret stops and turns around.

"Give it a thought."

Garret does not reply, but continues on his way out.

As soon as he is out of sight, the Director bungs his pen on the table. It clatters.

"Damn it!" he stifles.

He had obviously hoped the discussion would go smoothly. He is not sure where it all went wrong. But he feels he did his best to convince Garret. Maybe his expectations were too high. Maybe he thought his authority would make Garret nervous. But if he had observed the confidence on Garret's face all the while he was there, he would have realized that he came prepared.

In the parking garage, Garret hears from the left side, "Hello Garret," Agent Norman greets.

He has just alighted from his car alongside his colleague, Agent Stephanie. They are coming toward Garret. The greeting stops Garret in his tracks. He tries to clear the cloudiness around his face.

"You finally came," Agent Norman adds.

"Yeah," Garret replies.

"Pardon me: this (gesturing) is my colleague, Agent Stephanie..." He turns to Stephanie. "This is Garret Strong – the Einstein of our time."

"Hi," Agent Stephanie smiles and stretches forth for a handshake.

She has the looks of one in her late 20s. With bright blue eyes, thin lips and raven-black hair tied in a ponytail, she is more of a model than an agent.

"Hi!" Garret takes her hand.

"I believe your discussion with the Director went well?" Agent Norman intones.

"I believe so too."

Agent Norman appears to miss a blink with that response. He glances at Agent Stephanie.

"You were kidnapped by the Sinaloa Drug Cartel for the system," Agent Norman digresses. "We can work together to get them off your back..."

"At what cost? The T-system?"

"In as much as we would have loved that to be the price, but no - not that. I just realized that maybe we're pushing you too hard. Maybe we should take it slowly and let you decide on what you want to do."

Garret is silent, redolent of his words. First time someone is making sense around here and not throwing themselves on him, he thinks.

Agent Norman shoves his hand into the pocket of his coat and takes out his card.

"Here! Call me if you need my help."

Garret hesitates. He is not sure where this would lead them. But he hopes Agent Norman can be trusted. He stretches forth his hand and takes the card.

"Don't forget to call me," Agent Norman repeats. He turns to Agent Stephanie: "come on," he urges her.

Garret turns the card over in his hand, and then looks back at the agents as they walk towards the building elevators. He puts the card in his pocket and continues on his way.

CHAPTER ELEVEN: WHAT IS GOING ON HERE?

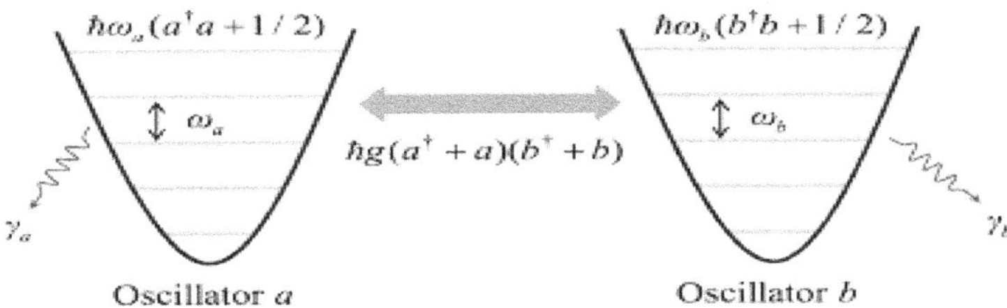

"What did the CIA want?" Judy asks, taking off her sweatshirt and throwing it on the small chair nearby. Garret sits on the couch and tries not to look, with a bottle of beer in her hand.

"Just what I thought – demanding that I sell the T-system to them," he replies, looking out the window.

"And what made them think you wanted to sell it?" Judy gets on the couch and covers her legs with the duvet.

"They think they're the government and can get whatever they want, maybe." Garret sips on the beer."

"You got that right." Judy stares at Garret, tapping her hand on the couch. "So, what's the next plan?"

"Honestly, I don't have any. I just hope everything resolves itself so I can get back to my life."

"Hmm! What about the T-system?"

Garret drinks from the bottle and clears his throat.

"It's somewhere safe," he answers.

Judy giggles. "I knew you weren't going to tell me that." She breathes out and tucks her hair behind her ear. "But seriously, I think you should take things easy…"

"Yeah…"

"Since the T-system is somewhere safe, the cartel and even the CIA will eventually lose interest with time. And even if the cartel somehow manages to get their hands on the system, they will need you to make it work. So it's not just about getting their hands on the system."

Garret pours down some of the beer.

"And I think…" Judy glides off the couch to where Garret is, putting her hand on his bottle of beer. "…you've had enough of this." She takes the bottle from him – there's not much left.

She gently plays the bottle on the corner table and sits on Garret's lap. With one hand pulling lightly on his hair and the other drawing invisible lines on his chest, the space between them is barely an inch.

"You need a good massage to de-stress you of the events of the past few days…"

She raises her face up at him. Their eyes lock in. Garret can feel the pull on his shirt. It is obvious Judy wants him to make the move first. Garret is not sure if this is right, or maybe it's his moral scruples coming to play.

But in less than a minute, their lips finally meet. They kiss softly. Garret wants to withdraw but Judy pulls him closer. She starts to take off his shirt as the kissing gets deeper and more passionate. Garret appears to have submitted to her seductions.

Their clothes are soon on the floor. Garret fondles her large firm breasts and sucks on them with undisguised desire. Judy lets off a soft moan. She gently guides Garret to the bed – their lips still locked in a torrid of sexual desires.

On the bed, they glide up and down each other's body, kissing and nibbling on every inch of flesh and making love. Judy dominates the action, twisting and whining up and down on Garret. Soft moans fill the air as they both revel in lusty pleasure. The bed is filled with fiery passion. Their groins are exploding with uncontrollable pleasure.

***

Meanwhile, at around 10pm, Ziko and his men return to Barnes' laboratory. It is with one intention – to tear down the building in search of the T-system. Mr. Barnes is in his office at this time. Through his window, he sees the jeeps drive up to the building. Quickly, he puts a call to the police. After the call, he dashes to a corner of the office and grabs his 12-gauge shotgun. It pays to be ready at all times, especially in these troubling times.

With a distinct sound he pumps the shotgun, locked and loaded. He then drops it on the table, pulls on his drawer and takes out five more shotgun shells. He shoves them into his pocket, and then grabs his 9 mm pistol and shoves a fully loaded magazine containing hollow point bullets. He chambers the pistol and storms out of the door.

While he was preparing his gun, Ziko and his men were forcing their way through the door breaking the lock with a heavy sludge hammer.

As soon as Mr. Barnes steps out of the office, he spots two of the men coming through the front door. He takes cover behind a laser scanner and opens fire at them. One of them has not fully gained entrance into the building, and that gives him the advantage to dash back outside. Fortunately, the man in front of him is hit several times. His lifeless body drops on the ground – his gun clatters beside him.

152

Mr. Barnes ceases fire and creeps toward the door. He wants to lock it from the inside. But halfway through, he hears footsteps. They seem to come from different directions. He hangs back behind a UV absorber system, with the muzzle of his shotgun directed at the door. He glances at the dead man on the floor. It doesn't seem like he will open his eyes ever again.

After a moment, everywhere falls silent again. It seems like the men have gone. But there's something – a smell. It is faint, yet Mr. Barnes' nostrils pick it up. It is that of fuel. Mr. Barnes raises his brow in thought. He surmises what the men have been up to outside.

He creeps toward the door. Suddenly, there's a loud shattering of skylight glass. The men have just broken in – almost through same point as the first time. Mr. Barnes heads for it, leaving the door.

As he sneaks past the broken glass, a shot is fired and hits the wall. Mr. Barnes finds cover behind a piece of equipment that looks like a dialysis machine. The equipment itself is riddled with bullets. The shooter clearly has his eyes on Mr. Barnes.

There's a light creak at the back door – someone is coming in. Mr. Barnes manages to navigate his way into the Clean Room. The whole lab has regained quiescence like there's no one in it.

The police siren breaks this silence. A breath of relief washes over Mr. Barnes. But the fight is far from over. As though the men heard him putting a call to the police, there are some of them outside waiting gallantly to engage the police in a shootout.

Mr. Barnes sneaks out of the Clean Room and repositions himself. Now he's headed for the front door. It is the only easy exit out of the building. He steals past a faulty quantum computer and crosses the door to Garret's section. But one more step forward, he hears the sound of a gun cocked.

"You lost, old man," a voice croaks from behind. "Drop your gun on the floor and put your hands behind your head slowly."

Mr. Barnes bends slowly to drop his gun. But at this time, the police vehicles arrive. This reboots his morale. He tries a quick turn to shoot at the man, but he gets a bullet to his right upper arm. The gun in that hand clatters on the ground as his yell rends the air. The thug capitalizes on that. He moves in and picks up the rifle. And then he smites Mr. Barnes at the back of his head with the butt of his gun. Mr. Barnes passes out.

"You got him," another man comes to the scene.

"Yeah."

"Great. Now let's get outta here…"

The other man carries Mr. Barnes onto his shoulder and lugs him toward the door. His colleague locates the container of fuel that had come in with. And then he begins to pour the fuel around the lab. At this time, the men outside have fully engaged the police in a war of bullets.

The man carrying Mr. Barnes waits by the door. His colleague soon comes and joins him. His job is simply to provide cover while the other man secures Mr. Barnes in the jeep.

"All right, come on," he calls.

He opens the door and begins to shoot at the police too. The men in the jeep intensify fire as they see them coming through the door. The other man lugs Mr. Barnes body straight into the jeep.

"Let's go! Let's go," one of them orders.

Another man in the jeep takes out an RPJ grenade launcher. His colleague quickly loads it. And then he aims it at one of the police vehicles and fires.

The police appear disoriented as the jeeps grind their tires against the ground and zooms off through another way. As they make it past the laboratory, one of the men throws a flare toward the entrance of the building; it lands on a heap of a carpet soaked with fuel. They placed cans of gasoline all thru the building – one of the things they were up to when it seemed to Mr. Barnes that they had gone.

The carpet ignites when the flare lands on it. The police may have tried to give a chase with the other vehicle, but the explosion that rocks the whole building as the fire spreads that holds them back.

The police maneuvered around debris that was on fire from the explosion. But by this time, the jeeps are far-gone.

***

Back at Judy's house, Garret lays on his back in bed, soundly asleep. Judy is not in the bed, and Garret has no clue he is alone.

However, the floor soon creaks lightly. Judy sneaks in. She has a gun with a silencer in her hand, and it's leveled at Garret. She is wearing a black combat trouser and a white sleeveless shirt. Obviously, she's been preparing for this moment.

"Wake up, Garret," she taps his foot. "Time to go."

Garret opens his eyes. The shock that hits him brings him to a sitting position at once.

"Judy? What's going on?" he questions, with a blurry vision from being suddenly awaken.

"It's time you returned to the cartel," Judy answers.

"You must be kidding, right?"

Judy shoots at the bed hitting the pillow next to Garret.

Garret moves his body slightly, and looks at the spot on the bed torn by the bullet. "… what is wrong with you, Judy?"

"Nothing is wrong with me. Like I said, it's time to get you back to the cartel. Get Dressed!"

"We can talk this through, Judy. You don't have to do this."

"The next bullet goes through your leg – Do you understand me?"

Garret gets off the bed – hands held out in submission. He picks up his trouser and shirt on the floor and begins to put them on, glancing at Judy at intervals. He is shocked that the girl he's building trust for has betrayed him. She's become a lot different from what he knew – that pretty girl with pure innocence in her eyes now wields a gun at him with the intent to kill. She's gone red in the face – eyes wild with violence. And with the way her hands are well positioned on the gun, it doesn't seem like it's her first time.

Garret has finished dressing up. Judy still has the gun pointed at him, while keeping a safe distance.

"Now move slowly to the door," she commands. "Let me see your hands in the air."

Garret does as she instructs, glancing over his shoulder.

"This is not right, Judy…"

"Shut up, and go on!" Judy blares.

But Garret grabs a comb on the table nearby and throws it at Judy. She fires a shot. Garret dives on the bed. As she turns her hand toward him, he throws a pillow at her. But the impact is not heavy enough to knock the gun off her hand. Garret knows. He moves in before she repositions and finally grabs her hands. A tussle for power breaks out between them. But Garret shows superior strength.

He delivers a punch to the hand holding the gun. It goes limp at once. The gun drops on the floor. He turns quickly and grips Judy by the neck. She turns to her side and gives Garret a blow to his ribs. He stifles a growl and releases the grip. Judy fires another kick to his chest. They both lose position at the same time and through a distance apart. While Judy is falling, her foot inadvertently kicks the gun. It slides across the floor and settles under the glass table somewhere at the center of the room – just between her and Garret.

"Who are you?" Garret asks, leaning against a chest of drawers, breathing hard – his hand on his side.

"My real name is Judy Rodrigez, you have met my father," Judy answers from the other end. She leans against the wall, not too far from the door.

"What? How?" Garret's face squeezes.

"Yes he is my father and I'm his loyal daughter. Things would be so easy if you would just let us have the T-system."

"You've been giving out information to them?"

"The easy part of the whole plan. After I killed my brother…"

"What?"

"Yes. He was one of us, but he betrayed my father by becoming an informant. He was caught. And to prove my loyalty to my family, I executed him with pleasure. Ziko learnt about your quest for research facilities. He kept a close watch on you and discovered that you were working at Barnes' Laboratory – That's when I applied for a PhD research assistant with Mr. Barnes. He could not resist. And so after I buried my brother, I kept a closer watch on you. We had your house and office bugged. I was also eavesdropping on your conversation with Mr. Barnes. I heard everything. And when you completed the project, I devised a way to bring you here so I can lead you back to my father."

"And what's in it for you?"

"Undetected delivery of our merchandise across the world – that's what pays the bills. We will make a billion dollars a day with undetected shipments. And for your information, we have Mr. Barnes now. You know what that means? Information!"

She gets on her feet and makes a dash for the gun, but Garret blocks her off. She sends a kick between his legs. He locks his knees – her shin collides with them. She punches Garret in the face. He staggers backward. Now she reaches for the gun again. But Garret regains his balance quickly and charges forward. She sends kick towards his face. This time, Garret catches her foot midair and throws her leg to the side. He grabs her by the arm pits, lifts her up and smashes her against the glass table. She groans, turning side to side.

As Garret pulls her up, her foot kicks the gun again to a different direction. On her feet, she smacks Garret's hands off her shirt and directs a punch to his neck, but Garret grabs her hand and twists it behind her. He pushes her forward and holds her against the wall. The gun is right next to her foot.

"Where is Barny? Where did you take him?" Garret interrogates, pressing her head against the wall.

"Why don't you surrender yourself and come with me to find out?" Judy giggles.

"I am not kidding, Judy. Where is Barny?" Garret presses her head harder against the wall and twists her arm higher.

"Screw you!"

Judy pushes her body against that of Garret's and flips her head to freedom. Another flip of the head backward lands on Garret's eyes – his grip weakens and Judy fights free. She picks up the gun. But before she levels it at Garret, a lightning fast fling of his leg plonks the gun out of her hand. It smashes against the window. Glasses shatter ceremoniously.

Garret grabs Judy and hurls her against the wall. Her head jams against it. She puts her hands on it in pain. Garret gives her no chance to breathe, for at this point he no longer fights reserved. There's anger mixed with adrenaline in him. He storms forward and grabs Judy again by the neck.

"Where is Barny? I won't ask again."

Judy is bleeding from her nose and the corners of her mouth. She spits blood in Garret's face. He shuts his eyes. And with one hand, he sends her flying across the room. She hits the wall, ricochets like a bullet and then lands on the bed, coughing and gasping for breath. Garret stomps to where the gun is and picks it up.

He points it at Judy. The anger has reached his face, making it reddish and swollen.

"Don't make me do this, Judy. Where have they taken Barny?" he intones, tightening his grip on the gun.

"There's... (coughs) only one way... (coughs again) to find out. Surrender and come with me!"

Garret charges to where she is and pulls her up. He pushes her against the wall and presses the gun to the back of her head.

"WHERE IS BARNY?" he bellows.

"Listen, Garret – they're here," Judy replies rather softly.

Garret stops for a moment – face crinkles.

"What are you talking about?" he asks.

Then it happens in a flash: the door swings open – Ziko's men storm in. And as they raise their guns at Garret, he takes a one-two step and dives through the window, not minding how far it is from the ground or where he will land.

The men come to the window and look down, but they don't see Garret anywhere. He must of landed on a row of plastic garbage cans.

"Come on," one of the men chivvies the orders.

They help Judy to her feet and out of the room.

Garret is hanging down a windowsill several meters above the ground. He gathers momentum and releases himself, grabbing the edge of the next windowsill below. Gasping for breath, he releases himself again. He hopes to grab the steel rod jutting out from a part of the wall. But instead, he crashes against what seems like a window hood made of trampoline and lands on the bare ground.

He gets on his feet at once and takes off.

"There!" he hears one of the men yell.

Several shots are fired in his direction, but he dodges them and keeps running. The men make a dash for their car. With Judy in it, the driver reverses frenziedly and goes after Garret.

Garret does not maintain the street path. He veers through another narrow alleyway. But somewhere in front, the alleyway is blocked off with a steel gate running from one end of the wall to another.

Garret gathers enough momentum as he runs. In three quick steps, he scales the steel gate and the wall. A powerful leap takes him to the roof of the building. From here, he sprints off – arms and legs swinging like pendulum. He has espied the car driving along the road, just next to the building.

He reaches the end of the roof and applies his brakes. The next roof is about 3 yards away. He takes some steps backward.

Having built up enough momentum in his muscles, he takes off. With one leap, he flies across the space – his hands get a firm grip on the edge of the wall, while the other parts of his body slam against it. Garret pushes himself up again and keeps running.

He leaps again and lands on a roof that's not too far from the ground. From here, he jumps again and lands back on the ground. He dashes through another path that leads through someone's backyard.

He navigates through a windy path and soon finds himself in a byway. He looks back, but does not see the car. They must have lost him, he thinks. Now he scuttles down the road, looking back at short intervals.

There's only one safe house in Garret's mind as he walks hastily along the road – his grandmother's house. It is about a two-hour walk located in a quaint suburb. Once he gets there he will make plans on how to rescue Barny. He may be going through torture now to disclose the whereabouts of the T-system or the laptop, Garret thinks. But he trusts Barny so much that he is certain he will not tell the cartel anything. He believes Barny will rather die than give out the information.

Garret's regret now is that he did not handle Judy hard enough for her to tell him where Barny is being held hostage. He feels he should have done more – applied more pressure in any way possible.

The only thing in his mind at this time is saving his best friend. And for that, he is willing to do anything.

CHAPTER TWELVE:
FOR EVERY ACTION THERE IS A REACTION

Grandma's house is a semidetached house. The house has been vacant for months since grandma was moved into a nursing home laying in a comma. A fence of flowers leads the walkway from the road to the patio. There's a lawn on the left side. On the right is a trail of fir trees. Chrysanthemum and sunflowers surround the building. There's no light outside the house - and it appears so inside.

Garret observes the surroundings. It seems safe here. He goes through the walkway, looking over the flowers. He must have become too cautious about his surroundings to think that Ziko's men will find him here. No one else knows about this place - just Mr. Barnes. And Garret is sure he won't tell on him.

Garret gets to the door - a thick door of pure mahogany. The key to the front door is under one of the many flower pants. The silver hinges squeak as he turns the handle and gently pushes the door inward.

He peeks in. His nose flares to the smell of dust. He gently goes through the door. With the door shut, he gropes across the wall on the right and finds the light switch - a click and the entire room becomes bright.

It's a spacious sitting room, with old dusty chairs. There's a fireplace on the left - next to it is a grand piano. A smile breaks off Garret's face at the sight of the piano. Grandma used to seat on the chair next to it and play her favorite song - 'Grandma's Hands' by Bill Withers.

He stares at the piano for a while and then looks up at the photo hung on the wall - it is that of grandma in her old age. She has a striking resemblance with Queen Elizabeth II - those small eyes and flabby cheeks - her eyes behind transparent glasses. She wears a gracious smile in the photo - a reflection of her heart. Garret goes closer and runs his hand across the photo. A myriad of his memories with grandma come whooshing into his head - one of which is his 4th birthday when she gifted him his first game box and the 5 jumpers she knitted herself. Garret beams as this memory sustains in his head.

Now his eyes go up the staircase. The floorboards creak under his weight as he ascends it to the bedrooms.

He comes to grandma's bedroom. There are more of her pictures here, and a four-poster. A spider had spun a perfect web across the room just like everywhere else in the house.

Garret breaks through the web to the chest of drawers somewhere across the wall. He pulls them out one after the other.

Now he turns to grandma's dressing table - her dressing mirror is still balanced atop the table. Garret pulls out the single drawer, and there it is - what he's been looking for - a small flip phone.

He takes it out and taps on it. But it does not come on. Garret surmises that the battery is probably dead. In the drawer, he finds the charger. He takes and pushes back the drawer. As he raises his head, his eyes find the mirror. He gazes at his reflection for a moment. The tiny cuts and bruises on his face represent a scientist that has been pushed to the wall.

He pours a deep breath and leaves the room, closing the door gradually to get a view of the room and the familiar smell of grandma perhaps for the last time.

Garret returns to the sitting room. He locates a wall socket and plugs in the phone. He goes to the chair by the piano and settles in it.

He stares at the keys like he has not seen something like them before. But his mind only momentarily wanders off to what Barny could be going through right now in the hands of those brutal men. At his age, he shouldn't go through that kind of torture. Garret's mind is sodden with sadness. But maybe playing a few notes on the piano will ease his emotions.

The only note he can think of is the favorite of the piano's owner – 'Grandma's Hand'. Having heard his grandma play it many times, there was no way he couldn't have learnt it.

He strikes a key. The sound echoes throughout the house, perhaps awakening the spirit of grandma's piano. He runs his finger down the keys. Adjusting his position, he places his fingers on the keys and plays, 'Grandma's Hand'.

His head is saturated with the memories of his grandmother as he plays the song. With his eyes closed and mouth stretched into a smile, he immerses himself in the melody. 'Grandma's Hand' was a song dedicated to all grandmas, and so at this point, Garret is sure in the company of other grandmas.

But as he strikes the last key, his mind wanders off to Barny again. He rests his hand on his thighs, gazing vacantly. He has to find a way to rescue Barny. He is not sure if he can do it alone, but he has to try at least. However, the fact remains that he does not even know where Barny is being held captive. He has to find him, nonetheless.

But even if he finds and rescues Barny, how does he fight all those men? He questions in his mind. He is reminded that he is not only dealing with the Sinaloa Drug Cartel but another group he has no idea about. The Asian must be combing the whole of DC for him now. He might have to enlist the help of the police and even the CIA for protection. All that will be after he rescues Barny. If only he can find his friends that trained alongside him with the Navy Seals, it will be a plus to his quest.

The voice in Garret's mind comes aloud. He mutters his thoughts to himself. Once the phone is charged he is going to call his best friend who trained with him as a Navy Seal Cadet and later became a Seal with Team6. But he soon loses to silence again, then to sleep right on the piano.

His senses are just about to leave the surroundings when he is awoken by the faint revving of a car. His eyes are thrown open at once. He gets off the chair and hurries to the window. In the thin grey light of the night, he spots a car in the far distance – it looks like the jeep of conveying Ziko's men. There's someone behind the steering wheel. And it looks like there are two other persons standing next to the car. Garret can't quite make out the rest of the details.

He observes the area and beyond. There's a feeling in him that something is about to happen. He goes to where the phone is plugged and unplugs. He takes the charge along too.

As he takes a step forward, he hears a light hissing sound, like something traveling through the air. Garret recognizes what it is. He strides across the floor and dives through the window, breaking the glasses.

Immediately he lands on the ground, an explosion rocks the whole building. He gets on his feet quickly and dives farther away. Burning woods and shards of glasses rocket across the sky as more parts of the house blows up.

Garret is now in a safe distance –it must appear to the thugs that nobody made it out alive. He watches as his grandma's house be reduced to rubbles along with the memories it carries. The only thing he has is the small phone in his hand. He looks at it, and then takes his eyes back at the burning building.

But the question is: how did the bomber find out that he was here? Could Barny have told them about the place? Garret is scuttling along the road now, farther from the scene while his thoughts run. He did not tell Judy about the place – he did not even mention anything about his parents let alone his grandma. Or did she put a bug on his clothes?

With that, he stops by the road and takes off his T-shirt worn over a round-neck. He checks the shirt, but finds nothing on it. He takes off the round-neck and there it is: a micro GPS bugging device about the size of a button. It must have been planted by Judy! Garret throws it on the ground and crushes it under his foot.

He runs as far away from the spot as possible – that way, Judy and her cohorts will not trace him. For where he will spend the night, he has no idea. It would have to be at the old farm house – but he fears his presence there might bring trouble – and that is where the T-system and his laptop are hidden. He sure as hell doesn't want that. He will continue walking until he finds a place safe enough to rest.

***

The morning comes with a response to Garret's wish. He passed the night in an abandoned warehouse. It could have been a hideout for criminals. But somehow, it was peaceful. Garret finally got to charge the phone. Garret text his good friend with an encrypted message.

Garret walks for about 4 hours into town heading for a specific cybercafé. A thought crossed his mind before he dozed off last night. He knows Barny's phone number off hand. Maybe he can track him with it. He doesn't think Barny will still have his phone with him though – but if it is being used by someone else, as long as it is on, he can track it.

As he looks around for that cybercafé, he sees his buddy standing next to his blue Audi.

Garret hastens his movement a bit.

"Hello Michael," he greets.

Michael looks to his side and removes his shades. He has light brown eyes and brown curly hair. He is tall, with broad shoulders and heavy chests. It will take a really massive hand to fully grab his neck. He's got a clean shave across his jaws. And his commanding personality is right about him.

"Yo, Garret, got your text."

They both shake hands – biceps bulging. He seems really happy to see Garret again.

"What's up with you, man? It's been a while, everything all right" he intones.

"Life is upside down right now and I need your help." Garret replies with a half-smile.

"Man, whatever you need." He looks down the road, and then back at Garret. "You want to get some breakfast? I know this great café just down the road. You can tell me what you need while filling your stomach."

"Okay." Garret shrugs.

"All right, get in the car."

Garret walks to the passenger's seat and opens the door. At least, he might not only get his request granted, but he's sure getting a free meal this morning.

The Audi soon pulls over in front of the cafe. Both men alight and walk through the door.

"This is one of my favorite places for breakfast," Michael reveals as they settle themselves at a table.

"Good for you," Garret replies, pulling a chair backward to sit. "I don't have a favorite. You know how it was back at the academy and then in Coronado."

"You can say that again." Michael's lips stretch upward in a sideway smile. He is glancing through the menu.

A middle-aged waitress soon arrives at their table with a cheerful smile on her face and a small jotter and pen in her hand.

"Good morning. What would you gentlemen like to have, please?"

"Get me some bacon, eggs and cheese sandwich," Michael orders.

"Okay." The waitress writes down his orders.

She turns to Garret.

"What would you like to have, sir?"

"Just bring me the same as his," he answers.

"Okay. Please relax. I'll be back shortly."

The waitress walks off.

"What is up, you look like a truck ran you over." Michael intones, keeping his glasses on the table.

"Everything has hit the fan. And I mean everything"

"That sounds like a pile or trouble?" Michael's brows fold. "What kinda trouble?"

Garret looks around the restaurant - other customers are busy with their meals at their tables - none of them is glaring at him or stealing suspicious glances.

He leans closer and rests his hands on the table. But as he is about to speak, the waitress returns with their order.

"Here you are, gentlemen." She places the plates and bottles of water and coffee in front of each of them.

Garret's salivary buds are filling the insides of his mouth with saliva as his eyes meet the scrumptious meal set before him.

"Enjoy your breakfast. Please do not hesitate to call me if there's anything else you may need," the waitress adds.

"Thank you." Michael replies.

"You're welcome." She walks away.

"Bon appétit, monsieur," Michael tells Garret.

"Bon appétit," Garret replies.

He picks up his fork and knife and stares at the food as if it's his first time seeing something like it. Michael is interested in what he was going to say before the waitress arrives.

"So, you were going to tell me about your world exploding?" he inquires as he eats.

Garret forks a piece of bacon into his mouth and looks up. He munches on the bacon and swallows quickly. He drinks some coffee and clears his throat - hands resting on the table.

"I developed a system that can teleport small objects..."

"A what?" Michael's jaw drops upon hearing that. He stops eating for a moment - eyes at Garret.

"Yeah, I call it T-system..."

"Yo bro, that's huge. I don't think anything like that has been invented."

"Not all. It's exactly what I've been working on since I was dismissed from the Navy..."

"That's a major breakthrough in science, man. You should be in the news right now."

"Unfortunately, I'm not. Now I have the Sinaloa Drug Cartel and even the CIA asking to buy the system..."

"And I guess you don't want to sell it to any of them?"

"No. And even if I will, to the CIA of course – not yet. I'm still working on the principles of the system."

Michael nods and puts the piece of egg on his fork into his mouth.

"So what exactly is the problem?" he asks.

"The cartel kidnapped me just so I could deliver the system to them, but I managed to escape. They've been after me ever since. The laboratory I worked in has been blown up, and Mr. Barnes, the owner of the lab, has been kidnapped. It seems like nowhere is safe for me. In fact, they blew up my granny's house blown last night in attempt to get me..."

"This is serious." Michael reclines on the chair. "And what are you doing to stop them?"

Garret exhales. "You and I know this is not a job for the police. I've been hoping to find one of the 12. And luckily, here you are. I'm hoping you'll help me get Mr. Barnes back. I had to send you an encrypted text message. I'm afraid all communication for me has been compromised.

Michael is silent, thoughtful of Garret's request. Garret gets back to eating. He glances at Michael at intervals, hoping he will agree. He has not held anything back about the cartel and his circumstances. He feels Michael won't betray him - it's a Seals brotherly trust that he knows he will not be betrayed. Garret believes that code will always bind them for life.

"I'll talk to Platini about this. I know he'd like to help. You know he's got this personal vendetta against drug cartels..."

"Yeah..."

Michael rests his hands on the table.

"You've got an idea where Mr. Barnes is being held captive?"

"No, but I'll find out."

"Okay. You said they took your phone. How do I reach you?"

"I got another one. I'll give you my number..."

The men get back to eating, and talking about the cartel and their operations as well as catching up on each other's news. Garret's wish has been granted. He not only has Michael to help, but Platini as well - two of the best during their combat and weapons training. Between Michael and Platini they have over 8 tours of duty in Afghanistan and Iraq. With them, Garret is assured of Mr. Barnes safe return.

***

Garret is at the cybercafé later in the day. With the system in front of him, he logs on to the website and inputs Barny's phone number.

But after a few seconds of loading, the system comes up with the notification: "phone number not found".

He tries again and again - the notification remains the same. He calls a worker at the cybercafé – a slim boy wearing a pair of glasses and resembling a nerd. Garret thinks he might know better, even though he already suspects the reason for the system notification.

"Hey man, I've been trying to track this number, but the system says, 'phone number not found'. Is there anything you can do?"

The boy takes over the keyboard and inputs the phone number. He clicks on 'track'. After the a few seconds, the same notification is displayed on the screen.

Garret watches as he types in another URL address. He inputs the phone number in the space provided and clicks 'track'. The same notification is shown after a few seconds.

The boy tries two more URL addresses. But the notification is the same.

"It's obvious, sir - the phone is switched off. Maybe you should try again later," the boy finally admits.

"All right, thank you."

Garret takes back the mouse and makes sure the phone number is not in the computer before he leaves.

He walks along the road, thinking of another way to find out to where Barny has been taken. His searching eyes meet every corner as he walks.

But then, as he walks past an arcade, he hears his name:

"Hey Garret." The voice is that of a man and comes in a low tone.

Garret turns around sharply in the direction. His eyes and those of George meet – his pupil constricts with surprise.

He walks to the arcade. George's eyes are dim – his saggy cheeks seem like they have a lead weight hanging down from them. The dullness in his eyes suggests the depression in his heart. That liveliness Garret once saw in him seems to have dampened.

"You don't look all right, George – what's wrong?" Garret inquires.

George is a bit reluctant to speak. Garret notices his lips trembling.

"What's going on, man?" he asks again.

"I'm sorry, Garret. I'm sorry…"

Now Garret is more curious than ever.

"Why are you sorry? What did you do?" he interrogates.

"They threatened my family, man. They said they were gonna kill my sister and my mum if I didn't tell them where the stuffs are. I'm sorry I betrayed you and Mr. Barnes."

Garret can already put together what he means. But he wants to know more.

"I don't understand, George. Who threatened your family? And what stuff are you talking about?"

"They asked me to keep a close watch on Mr. Barnes. I didn't want to betray you – I didn't want to betray Mr. Barnes. But they threatened to kill my family. They knew all about me. So that night, I followed Mr. Barnes to the old farm house where he hid the T-system and the laptop in the barn. Later, I went back to them and led them to the farm house. But I only showed them where the T-system was. The laptop is still safe there. Since then, my conscience has been tormenting me – and I've been looking everywhere for you. I'm really sorry, man."

Garret has turned crimson in the face. His jaws are clenched tightly as he stifles the anger building up inside of him. His hands have been made into a fist, but he just can't release them on George. In the height of his anger, there's a sense of reasoning. Anyone in George's situation would have done the same. But the fact that the cartel now has the T-system shoots his anger to an inferno.

Garret lands George an eye-reeling punch on the face. The impact is so powerful he flung his hand as he himself felt the pain. George staggers backward and falls to the ground. He remains in position to nurse the pain and dismiss the twinkles in his eyes. Overridden with contrition, he does not attempt to fight back. Garret's chest is rising and falling heavily. He flings his hand again and turns the other way – eyes shut. George is now bleeding from his mouth and nose. He takes out his handkerchief and cleans up.

After about a minute, Garret turns again at George. His anger appears to have subsided. His face is starting to regain its color – his pupils returning to normal dilation. George too manages to get on his feet.

"I'm sure you know Mr. Barnes has been kidnapped by the cartel." Garret speaks – some fragments of his anger are still etched in his voice.

"Yes, I know." George clears his throat.

"Then you should know that by now, he'll be going through intense torture to show them how to use the system. But you know what: he can't because he doesn't have the formula. The men will not believe him, and they will keep torturing him."

George glances up at Garret. It seems to dawn on him the depth of the consequences of his betrayal.

"I'm dreadfully sorry, man," he expresses. "I wish there was a way I can make things right."

Garret glares at him. He has nothing much to do or say to George now. He not only has Barny to rescue but the T-system as well.

"Do you know where Mr. Barnes has been taken?" he inquires.

"No, I don't," George answers after a moment of thinking. "But maybe you can get the information from one of the men."

"Where do I find them?"

"At X-R clubhouse."

Garret frowns. "Where is that?"

"Not too far from Supreme Mall. You can hear the music from the mall – or I can take you there, if you want." George sniffs and cleans off a drop of blood from his nose.

"I'll find it."

George recoils – eyes unfocused.

"Judy is not the person you think she is. Better be careful around her." As Garret said these words, he leaves George at the spot and walks away.

George would have loved to know more, but he wouldn't dare ask. Garret is too infuriated to give an answer. Whatever he does with this information is now entirely up to him.

***

The old farmhouse is a small cabin in an open cornfield. It has windmills at different points in the field. There's an abandoned truck in front of the barn. Having been out here since Garret's grandfather died 6 years ago, it appears its fault is way beyond a quick repair.

At 8pm, Garret traipses along the narrow path to the cabin. The last time he was here was 5 years ago, with grandma to help sort thru his grandfather's things. Somehow, his parents have managed to keep the place functioning – paying workers to work on the field. The land was to sentimental to sell.

The double door of the barn clanks open. The smell of corn mixed with dust accompanies the zephyr of air that hits Garret's nostrils. As he comes through the door, hordes of bats flap from one end of the cabin to another – some escaping through the door. Garret gives way for them. It's dark in here. Garret opens the doors allowing sunlight to enter the room

175

The light reveals some of the working tools – a wheelbarrow, spades, rakes, watering can, hose and others. But most importantly, there's no one in here.

Garret walks to a corner of the barn on the right side next to a horse stable. He crouches, looking for something. The ground is covered with wisps of wheat and corn. But Garret sees a bare spot. It shows indeed that someone has been here.

Garret removes three of the floorboards to reveal a square pouch about the size of a chessboard and depth of about three feet. The T-system was hidden under the floorboards of the barn.

Underneath the floorboards he only finds a piece of black cloth. He deduces that this is where Mr. Barnes had hidden the T-system before it was stolen.

He puts the floorboards back in place and goes to another corner of the barn on the far left – next to a heap of corn. He removes the floorboards and finds his laptop wrapped in a piece of black cloth.

He takes it out and observes every part of it. It seems untouched. He puts back the floorboards and then goes to sit on the porch of the farmhouse.

He powers on the laptop to make sure the formula and every other detail is still in it. He will be here the whole night, in hopes that he will get Michael's call in the morning.

CHAPTER THIRTEEN:
THEY DON'T STAND A CHANCE

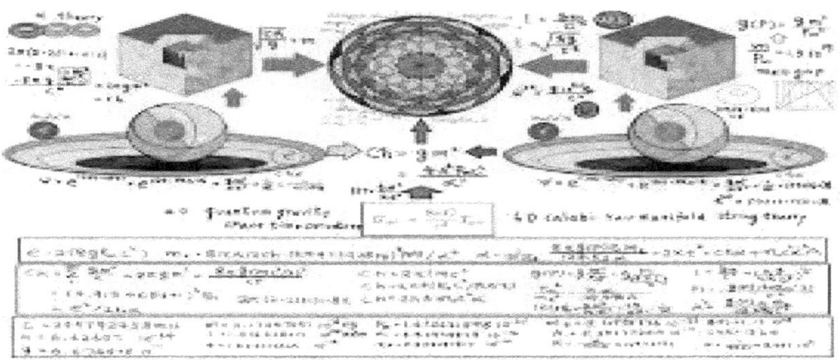

Mr. Barnes is tied to a steel chair inside a room. Shining only and around the spot is a dull red light. Every other part of the room is faintly illuminated by reflections from the lights outside. The building has other parts, but this room is the central unit. Standing around are thugs, with hands on their rifles.

The corner of Mr. Barnes' left eye is swollen. His lips are broken and dropping blood. The blood from his nose appears to have dried up on his upper lip. He has been stripped of his shirt. Now he wears his undershirt. There are bruises around his chest and abdomen, suggesting that he's been going through a lot of anguish. His head is bent low. At a glance, one can tell that he's barely hanging on.

The clank somewhere in the hall echoes loudly. Footsteps are approaching toward Mr. Barnes. The faint reflections soon reveal Ziko, Judy and another man. There's quickness of limbs now that he has the T-system. His smile has returned. Now he wears it across his face like a self-satisfied wizard. Judy has cleaned up, but still has the wounds from her fight with Garret.

"Hey, old man," Ziko calls – they are standing in front of Mr. Barnes. He turns to a thug standing nearby. "Get him."

The thug comes and pulls Mr. Barnes by his hair. He shrieks in pain and raises his head. He can barely open his left eye. He doesn't seem surprised at the sight of Judy. He's probably seen her before now.

"We've tried all we can to get the system to work. Judy has applied her expertise. We've contacted our best research teams across the world. But none of these people have been able to come up with the right formula to make the system work. Now I am made to understand that there's a laptop that contains the formula we've been looking for. I need you to tell me where it is."

Mr. Barnes coughs and shakes his head free from the grasp of the thug behind him. "I don't know about any laptop," he answers – his voice has become flaky.

Ziko smiles and comes and crouches at Mr. Barnes' feet.

"I know you do, and trust me, I don't have the luxury of time to continue asking…" He turns to the thug. "Get me the baton."

Mr. Barnes sighs. Although his body may not be strong enough to take more beatings, he just can't imagine betraying Garret. He is ready to die with whatever information he has. Ziko is willing to oblige him, although in a slow and pitiless way.

His hands get hold of the baton. With that creepy smile on his face, he walks around Mr. Barnes.

"You're pretty loyal to your boy, I must confess. At the same time, you are the most foolish man I have ever met…"

He smites Mr. Barnes' abdomen with the baton. He groans in pain, coughing out blood from his mouth.

"Tell me where the laptop is hidden."

"I don't know."

Ziko slams the baton on his belly again and again. Mr. Barnes groans in excruciating pains. Judy stands with a plain countenance – not a hint of remorse.

Ziko stops the attack for a moment to adjust his suit. Judy then walks to Mr. Barnes. She stares at his wounds and stretches her hand to touch his head. Mr. Barnes shakes his head dismissively.

"Why don't you tell us where the laptop is and save yourself this torture?" she advices him.

"Rot in hell!" Mr. Barnes huffs and spits on her.

She closes her eyes and swallows hard.

"That's where you're going to be soonest." She steps backward. "Hit him harder until he talks."

"With all pleasure." Ziko steps forward with a leer. "I'm gonna ask for the last time: where is the laptop?"

"You are ridiculously dumb!" Mr. Barnes spits.

The smile on Ziko's face vanishes at once. He delivers one final shot to Mr. Barnes' head. He fades instantly…

***

At around 10pm, Garret is in front of Supreme Mall – a busy area in the heart of the city. Just like George told him, he can hear the music from the club from here. The X-R clubhouse is about 100m away.

Garret kicks off toward the club. All through the day, he kept thinking of what Mr. Barnes could be going through. He still believes he will not give up the location of the laptop – although he himself has hidden it somewhere else. All he hopes is that he finds Mr. Barnes in time.

Neon lights display the name of the club across the building. Garret is a stone throw away. He walks through the warm white lights into the cover of the dark. But just as he crosses a small wooden fence, he gets a kick to the head – so hard he is sent flying in the air and crashing back against the fence.

He quickly scrambles on his feet – fists clenched – just then, the Asian menace from before shows himself. He is dressed just like before, with his glasses even in the dark.

"We meet again," he croaks.

Garret tightens his fists. His face has turned scarlet – eyes wild and ready. He is suddenly sated with these persistent attacks and hopes to end it with this man right now.

"I'm gonna ask you one question: who sent you to get me?"

"You will find out once I take you to him."

Garret takes a fighting position – eyes locked on the man. For all the time he trained in the Navy, it is time to show it. He will not be subdued by this man.

The man charges forward, sending another kick to Garret's head. He blocks it off and falls backward a bit. The man pushes closer again and begins to throw blows from all sides. Garret is quick enough to defend every one of them. The assassin aims at his face, but Garret bends out of the way and grabs his hand – he turns sharply and throws the man on his side.

The assassin gets on his feet again. Achieving this throw gives Garret more confidence. Now he is more agile than ever. The man storms forward again. Garret directs a kick to his side, leaps in the air and gives him a knee to the face. He pushes against the sands and regains his balance.

Garret goes for another kick, but the man catches the leg and throws it aside. He grabs Garret by his collar, lifts him in the air and hurls him against what's left of the wooden fence.

Before Garret gets on his feet, the assassin moves in. But as he bends to drag Garret up, he is locked in a choke. Garret wraps his arms around his neck, pressing his Adam's apple against his knee. The man struggles to fight free. Garret squeezes tighter, shaking vigorously at intervals.

But with immense strength, the man lifts Garret while he is still in that position and slams his back on the ground. Garret releases his grip and a groan. The assassin falls backward, coughing and gasping for air.

He rubs his neck and storms back again. He mounts on Garret and begins to throw punches at his ribs and face. Garret can only block a few of them. Satisfied, the assassin gets up.

Garret rolls about on the ground in pain. The man grabs the wooden chair by the side, and hangs nearby as Garret struggles to get back on his feet.

As soon as he does, the man smashes a wooden chair against his abdomen. Garret groans, with his hands on his belly. That exposes his back and the man cashes in on that. He slams the wooden chair on Garret's back. He groans again and staggers forward.

"Let's finish this," the man declares.

He rushes in to smash Garret's head with pieces of the wooden chair, but Garret dodges it. He flings the chair backward toward Garret's face, but Garret catches it. He punches the man's bicep – his arm falls weak – the chair falls off his hand. Garret leaps up and gives him a knee on his lower jaw. He falls backward. Garret runs and delivers another kick right on his forehead. The man falls farther and lands on a pointed piece of wood. Garret lands on the ground and charges forward again. But then he stops halfway, seeing blood pour from the man's mouth. The stake has driven through his chest. Garret watches as his lifeless head falls to the side.

As Garret takes a step toward the clubhouse his phone chimes in his pocket. He takes it out. It's a call from Michael.

"Hey man, I've got Platini in the game. Where do we meet up?" Michael intones.

"I'll be at Supreme Mall in 30 minutes," Garret replies.

"Okay. We'll be there…"

Garret looks again at the body of the assassin – blood dripping from his chest. Sad he didn't get to find out who sent him. Surely his boss will come for revenge. Garret hopes he will be ready when that time comes.

He looks up at the clubhouse, off he goes.

He ghosts through the dark and gets to the door. It's loud and stuffy in here – cigarette smoke and the warmth from the clubbers. Garret stands by the door, looking to single out his target. He doesn't have to alert everyone – just find his target, knock him out and carry him off.

And from where he is, he spots one of Ziko's men – the one that got shot blankly by his fellow comrade. He is making his way out of the hall through the door on the right side. As soon as he steps out of the hall, Garret follows.

Garret leans on the edge of the building, watching as the man smokes and bounces to a corner a few yards away from the building. He has his hands around his groin – obviously going for a pee.

He gets to the desired spot and unzips his trouser. While he passes urine, Garret creeps closer and closer. He is no longer covered by anything – the man will see him clearly if he looks back. For that, Garret runs faster.

The man bounces on the spot and zips up his trouser. Immediately he turns, Garret smacks his neck with the edge of his hand. The man passes out.

Garret looks back at the 90s Cadillac in front of the clubhouse, idling for the valet to park the car. He had planned his exit with it when he first saw it.

He scuttles to it and looks inside after the valet leaves. Graciously, the valet left the key in the ignition. Garret dashes in quickly and drives the car back to where the thug is. He lugs him up and puts him in the trunk.

Back into the car, he reverses frenziedly and heads toward Supreme Mall. Now he has the man to tell him all that he needs to know. With his friends to back him up, he will rescue Barny and the T-system.

***

The thug has been tied to a chair in the old farm house barn. He is surrounded by Garret and his men. Platini is of a regular height. The last time he visited the gym was probably yesterday's morning. He is wearing a body-hugging shirt that shows his bulging chest and biceps. He is bald, with a neck almost as wide as that of Michael's. His hands are about the size of a dustbin lid – only basketball players are expected to have such hands. And when he makes a fist, it's as though he's wearing a boxer's glove.

Their captive is awake and has been yelling: "let me go". Platini has promised he will do just that if only he gives them the information they need.

Now Garret stands in front of the thug – Michael and Platini leaning against the wall, watching.

"I'm sure you know why we did not bother to seal your mouth?" Garret asks.

The thug does not answer – he just glares at Garret.

"Well, in case you don't, it is because it's pointless. This is a farmhouse – far away from the heart of the city. I'm sure you've been here before, looking for the T-system. Now you have it. But I want it back. I also want my friend back. So I ask: where are you guys keeping him?"

The thug smirks. "I'm not telling you anything."

Garret is quiet for a moment. He walks closer to the man and bends so that their eyes meet in a straight line.

"Yes, you will. I assure you." He stands back. "I'm gonna ask again: where is my friend being held hostage?"

"Go to hell! I won't tell you any…"

Garret sends a massive right hand across his chin. His face is thrown to the side. He stays in position for a while. By the time he raises his face, Garret is walking to where the some of the tools are packed.

After a few seconds of searching, Garret finds what he is looking for – a hand drill. He comes and stands before the thug.

He powers the device on. The thug's face turns pale. His head is pushed backward – eyes torn with terror.

"Now, I'm gonna ask again: where is my friend?" Garret reiterates.

"I – I told you, I'm – I'm not telling you any…thing." That sound sure sent chills down his spine.

Garret powers the device again and drops the drill bit on the thug's thigh. A loud continuous growl breaks the air. The drill tears through flesh and muscles, almost reaching the thigh bone. Blood is spilling from the spot. The thug screams a horrific scream.

Garret withdraws the drill. The thug gasps and yells. He is panting for breath. And then he looks down at the narrow hole that has been drilled through his thigh. It is clogged up by blood – he would have been seeing his thigh bone but there was too much meat and blood.

"The next hole will be made through your eye," Garret speaks. "One more time: where is my friend held captive?"

The thug continues to groan, pretending like he didn't hear the question. Garret understands that tactic.

He powers the drill again and moves closer. Slowly, he projects the drill bit toward the thug's eye. Michael is holding his head in position. The thug continues to yell as the drill gets closer and closer to his eyes.

Just an inch close, he breaks: "Okay, okay, I'll tell you – I'll tell you."

Garret withdraws the drill and turns it off. The thug pants for breath. He is still bleeding from his thigh and no one is bothered about that.

"King's Warehouse – that's where he is – that's where the system is…"

"King's Warehouse? Where is that?"

"I think I know where it is, man…" Michael cuts in.

The longer Mr. Barnes stays at that warehouse, the closer he is to his death. Garret will not let that happen. And tonight, he and his men will storm the place. Platini and Michael have brought an arsenal of weapons, ready for World War 3.

CHAPTER FOURTEEN: TIME TO GET SOME!

$$T^2 - \sum_{i=1}^{3} X_i^2 = t^2$$

Michael scuttles across the parking lot on the right side of the building. There's a thug standing next to a light post in the front. His eyes are locked on. Platini makes his way from the left. He has his eyes on the thug standing next to a trashcan. Garret takes cover behind a car. From here, he sizes up two of the thugs standing not too far away from the front door.

As it is an unofficial duty, Michael and Platini are not with their official guns. They only have their personal pistols tucked down their waists and their AR over their shoulders. The plan is that the thugs will provide them with the weapons they need throughout the invasion so they are traveling very light. With their boots and livid combat trousers, they are ready to penetrate the building and rain havoc upon the cartel.

Michael creeps up behind the thug and twists his neck at once. He drops on the ground. He drags his body and hides it behind a car. Platini strangles his man from the back.

With both sides clear, Michael and Platini advance. Garret creeps closer and reveals himself to the men. He has his pistol tucked to the back of his waist.

"Who are you? Stop right there!" the men bellow.

Garret raises his hand in the air in submission as the men march closer. They quickly level their guns at him when he comes into the light.

"Get your hands behind your head. Turn around!" the men bark orders.

But a few steps from Garret, Michael and Platini grab them from behind. Michael snaps the neck of one – Platini cuts the throat of the other. They both drag their bodies off and hide them on the side of the building.

With the front part of the building secured, Michael and Platini arm themselves with the thugs' guns.

"Remember the plan, guys?" Garret says.

"Rodger that," Platini answers.

"Good. Let's go."

Platini advances from the left - Michael from the right. Garret heads for the front door.

He gets to it and takes a deep breath - then he pushes the door inwards and walks through.

Immediately the thugs see him, they all scramble to their feet, pointing their guns at him. Garret has his hands behind his head, glancing around. He is in the central room of the warehouse. And looking toward the far end, he sees Mr. Barnes. He is still alive - although not conscious at this time.

One of the men counts his steps closer to Garret. With one hand on his gun, the other searches Garret. He takes out the pistol tucked to his waist.

"Now move," he pushes Garret forward, toward a table at the center of the room.

One of the other thugs walks through a door, to the inner rooms. Garret continues to glance at Mr. Barnes who has not moved at all since he came in.

After about a minute, Garret hears footsteps approaching. Shortly after, Sr. Ramirez walks through the door, alongside Ziko and Judy.

"Mr. Strong! We meet again," Sr. Ramirez intones. He comes and stands at the steel table, opposite Garret. "Honestly, I was surprised when my associate told me that you are here at this late hour. Considering the way, you left the last time, I didn't think you would walk back in here on your own, knowing full well that I might kill you right on the spot."

"No, you won't," Garret replies. "You need me alive to help you activate the T-system. You need me to get the formula and have the T-System operational."

Sr. Ramirez cocks a brow. "Hmm, clever!" he comments. "But don't you think I might kill you right after you provide me with everything I need?"

Garret does not answer.

"I take your silence for affirmation. But I'm curious, Mr. Strong: why exactly are you here? Surely, you couldn't have just walked in here for nothing."

Garret is quiet for a moment, before speaking.

"I came to activate the T-system and give you the working formula. In return, you will let my friend go." Garret's eyes are focused - face hardened with anger.

"And you really think I'll believe that?"

"No, I don't. But if you've ever had a friend who means more than anything in the world to you, you would believe what I've just told you."

"Hmm..." Sr. Ramirez walks to where Garret is and stands by his side. "I like you, Garret Strong. Your intelligence impresses me. We can work together. I can set up an ultramodern laboratory for you. With your intelligence, we will rule the world..."

"Thank you. But I am not interested. Please bring the T-system so I can activate it. I'll also need a laptop to write you the formula."

"I see..."

Sr. Ramirez gazes at Garret for a while and then gives Ziko a nod. Ziko turns back and walks through the door.

"I really would have liked to be friends with you, Mr. Strong," Sr. Ramirez continues while they wait for Ziko. "But you are stubborn. Nevertheless, I must thank you for inventing something that will make my business a lot easier. With your invention, I can send a parcel anywhere in the world without the DEA and the FBI or any other Narcotics Agency confiscating my shipments. And trust me, I would have offered you a lot of money for it..."

Ziko returns with the T-system carried by two of his men. He also has a laptop in his other hand. He gently puts them on the table in front of Garret. All the thugs have their guns pointing at Garret.

"Okay, Mr. Strong - here you are. Do your thing so we can all go to bed? It's late."

Garret opens the laptop and powers it on the he stops and looks up at Sr. Ramirez.

"Is something wrong, Mr. Strong?" Sr. Ramirez asks.

"What assurance do I have that you will let my friend and I walk out of here alive after I activate the system and write the formula?"

Sr. Ramirez smiles. "I have lasted long in this business because I am a man of my word. You have nothing to fear, Mr. Strong."

"I don't believe you."

Garret pulls out a knife from his boot, yanks Sr. Ramirez closer and puts it to his neck. It happened so fast the thugs didn't see it coming.

"Hey, hey, hold your fire," Ziko orders.

Now they all have their guns cocked and leveled at Garret and Sr. Ramirez. Garret backs away from the table, dragging Sr. Ramirez with him.

"You don't know who you're messing with, Mr. Strong," Sr. Ramirez gloats.

"Shut up!" Garret blares. "Now drop your guns. DROP IT!"

Ziko nods at the men. They all slowly lay their guns on the ground.

"Come on in, guys," Garret calls.

Michael and Platini storm in, pointing their guns at the thugs.

"Get Mr. Barnes!" Garret gestures his head toward the far end of the room.

Michael goes for him while Platini gathers the guns on the floor.

"You really think you've outsmarted me, Mr. Strong!" Sr. Ramirez speaks again.

"Shut up!" Garret presses the knife deeper into his neck. He yelps.

Platini carries the bag on the table. Michael is thumping toward the door, carrying Mr. Barnes on his shoulder.

"Now get down on the floor - all of you," Garret orders.

They hesitate.

"He said get down," Platini storms in, slapping and kicking them down on their knees, making sure they are in a submissive position.

He searches all of them, including Ziko and Judy and retrieves the pistols tucked down their waists. Now he packs all the guns and throws them far away from the building one by one.

As they are exiting the building a shot is fired in their direction. Platini with his sharp reflexes avoided a bullet to his head. He shoots at the thug, creating a chance to take cover behind the doors entrance.

This moment of distraction disrupts the whole operation. Michael, still carrying Mr. Barnes, grabs the laptop and heads for the door. Another thug runs out through the other door. He wants to shoot at him. Garret has no choice but to give up holding Sr. Ramirez hostage. He hurls the knife at the thug. Like a dart, it pierces through his head. Ziko runs to the pile of guns in the corner of the room. Garret and Michael try to run out of the room, but Ziko stops them.

"One more move and I'll have your brains splattered everywhere."

Garret and Michael stand on the spot. Some of the other thugs run inside to get their guns – others wait for them.

"Drop the laptop on the table and the man on the floor," Ziko orders.

Michael hesitates.

"Don't make me say it again."

Michael thumps forward and drops the laptop on the table and lays Mr. Barnes on the floor. At this time, he is awake – just a handful of life left in him.

Platini storms back in, pointing his gun at Ziko. At the same time, the other thugs return – armed, and with extra guns to spare for Judy and the others.

"Give it up, boys – you're outnumbered and outgunned," Sr. Ramirez warns, cleaning the blood from his neck wound.

"Lay your weapons on the floor," Ziko orders.

Garret turns to his men and gives them a nod. Slowly, Platini bends to put his gun on the floor. Michael's gun has been hanging down his neck. He removes it gently and bends to drop it on the floor.

But halfway through, Platini opens fire on the guard next to him. As his inanimate body drops on the floor, Garret quickly dives on the floor to pick up a Ak-47 and starts shooting. Sr. Ramirez cleverly weaves his way out, under the cover of his guards and escapes through the back door. Michael takes cover behind the table and picks up another AK from a dead thug. Ziko and some of the men take cover behind large cartons and wooden crates in the section that branches off the central warehouse. Bullets fly in every direction. Platini covers for Garret while he secures the T-system.

But as he grabs for the T-system, he has no idea that Judy is somewhere behind the table. Judy shoots at Garret, but Mr. Barnes, with what is left of his strength dives in the line of the bullets. They tear mercilessly through his back and he falls next to Garret. Platini turns sharply and riddles Judy with bullets. Her lifeless body drops on the floor.

Garret is struck with shock at what just happened. Platini and Michael engage Ziko and the others in a war of bullets. A car screeches to a stop outside. Agents Norman and Stephanie storm out. They did not come through the front door, but quickly dash toward the back door.

"CIA! Cease fire!" Agent Norman bellows from behind.

It doesn't seem like anyone heard him. Shots come from the second floor as CIA and FBI swat team descend from above.

"Drop your weapons, you are surrounded!"

This time, Ziko and two of his men hear the order. They raise their guns in the air in submission. Michael and Platini have stopped shooting too.

"Drop your guns slowly on the ground and kick them aside," Agent Norman orders.

The men, including Ziko do as they are instructed. Agents move in and cuff all of them.

Mr. Barnes is gagging and jerking lightly, spurting blood from his mouth. He still has some life left in him – this gives Garret the hope that the he can still be saved.

"Someone call an ambulance!" Garret yells – voice quavering. "Don't die on me, Barny, please," he cries.

He carries Mr. Barnes outside, toward the car. But on his way, he notices that Mr. Barnes' head is thrown backward. He quickly lays him on the ground.

"Don't you dare die on me, Barny! Barny!" he calls and shakes Mr. Barnes' body. But it's starting to get cold. He is has succumbed to his wounds.

Garret shivers with grief. His cheeks are flushed – his eyes are bloodshot. Michael and Platini come out of the building. Their faces swell with sadness as they gaze at Mr. Barnes' body, and Garret sobbing deeply next to it.

"Come on, man," Platini bends over and pats gently on Garret's shoulders.

He helps Garret on his feet while Michael lugs Mr. Barnes' body up his shoulder.

It is the end of a loyal friendship – the end of a perfect father-son relationship. The T-system is secured but at what cost? Garret can't get his eyes off Mr. Barnes' body. Every bruise on his body – every mark – his swollen eye all tell him how much he must have endured for the sake of loyalty.

Garret can feel his heart hammering against his chest. His whole body shakes – even his knees can no longer support his weight. Platini keeps him standing. He watches behind a mist of tears as his best friend's body is taken to the car…

CHAPTER FIFTEEN: KA-BOOM

It's two weeks after the showdown between Garret and Sinaloa Drug Cartel. Mr. Barnes has been buried. It was probably the worst days of Garret's life. He plunged into dark depression for a few days – drinking and sulking. The memories of him and Mr. Barnes kept flooding into his head. Agents Norman and Stephanie and his friends, Michael and Platini were there to help him through the days. But the most effective help he got was from time. Eventually, he started to heal.

On the first day of the third week, he is in the Director's office again. It is time to do what he thinks is right. The relief on the Director's face upon seeing him in his office is undisguised.

"I am here for the proposal," Garret declares – his face is still heavy in grief.

"You know my office has always been open for this discussion," the Director replies. "I am glad you are back."

Garret stays quiet for a while before speaking.

"First, the system is no longer to be referred to as 'T-system'. It is now to be called, 'B-system'…"

"Okay. And may I ask what the 'B' stands for?" the Director asks.

"Barnes."

"Oh…" the Director raises his brow.

It is not far-fetched the reason Garret renamed the system. It is in memory of his loyal friend who died protecting the system and Garret.

"Secondly, I will give up the B-system and all the formula for 10 billion dollars initial payment and a 100 million dollar annual salary. Remember, if I am threatened by the government in any way in the course of keeping this agreement, I will send 10 emails containing the formula of the B-system to 10 foreign governments and to every drug cartel. This is my proposal. If you agree to it, then we have a deal."

The Director exhales deeply. He stares at Garret for a while, thinking of the terms of the proposal. Garret keeps his eyes on the globe ball on the table.

The Director leans closer on the table.

"I would have agreed to your proposal this minute, but 10 billion dollars and your salary is too much for a one-man decision, regardless of the fact that I am the Director. The money is not leaving my account but that of the government's." He exhales again. "I will have to talk to some people who are also involved in this. I assure you that I will do my best to convince them to agree to your proposal. I will get back to you after that."

Garret raises his eyes at the Director. "All right then. I'll be waiting for your call."

"And I must add that for the government to agree to make the payment, you must have the B-system tested. That is the only way we can sure it's operational." With a hard stated fact from the Director.

Garret exhales gently and nods. "Okay."

He gets on his feet. The Director gets up too. They both shake hands and then Garret leaves the office. The Director pulls his seat closer and sits back. His eyes are at the door as he knocks the pen in his hand rhythmically on the table. He thinks of the power Garret has now with the B-system. Anyone who has the capability to transport material through teleportation can literally control the world even in the comfort of their homes. Nothing and no one is safe. However, he doesn't think Garret knows this yet or does he?

As Garret makes his way out of the premises, he sees someone on the other end of the road – it looks like Ziko. He tries to get across the road, but he is blocked off by a school bus.

By the time the school bus crosses the road, the person is no longer there. Garret crosses to the side and looks around. He runs to the alleyway nearby, but he finds no one.

Now he stands in the alleyway, thinking whether it's a mirage or not. But he is sure it was Ziko. He has that smile on his face, and wearing that ugly blue suit. Could he have been released from the jail – or maybe even escaped? Whatever the answer is, Garret is once again reminded that the war will never be over.

***

In due time, with the help of some cartel informants in Mexico, the CIA discovers Sr. Ramirez' location. He is hiding on a remote island off the Mexican shores. He knows that the American Government is looking for him so he tries to become a ghost. His hiding spot is discovered to be a Hacienda fortified 20 miles off shore. Inside the Hacienda it's more like a bunker. The island is completely self-sufficient and manned with a small army of loyal men, he feels very safe there. But he soon runs out of luck.

The room is set for Garret to prove to the government that the B-system works. The B-system has been placed on a metal stand. Garret is standing in front of the system with his laptop and a phone next to him. The cell phone will serve as a detonator. Top government officials – ten of them, including the Director of CIA, Director' of the DOD and FBI along with the Vice President and other cabinet leaders surround Garret.

The aim of the demonstration is to destroy Sr. Ramirez' hideout and perhaps eliminate Sr. Ramirez in the process. Garret willingly accepted the task, as it gives him an opportunity to avenge Barny's death.

Garret sets the C-4 explosive in the system portal. Attached on top of the C-4 package is a small micro camera that will transmit all activity. The men watch expectantly, glancing at each other. He takes it one step at a time so the men will not miss the process.

As soon as Garret turns on the system from his laptop, green lights start to glow and then lights spread around the C-4, giving a light whirring whooshing sound with a circle of sparks. Garret checks the predetermined location with the GPS coordinates.

With the system fully loaded and ready, Garret glances up at the men. The Director gives him a nod. He then presses a computer key on the laptop. The green and white swirling light consumes the C-4. And in a moment, it disappears. The officials' faces are startled at what they have witnessed – one of them cocks a brow and glances at the others.

With the phone in Garret's hand, he monitors the hideout through the camera. The micro-camera monitors the room with its fish-eye lens. The C-4, teleported what seems to be the center of a conference room table in Sr. Ramrez's Hacienda.

After a few minutes, Garret spots Sr. Ramirez walk into the conference room with about five of his men. Garret was hoping that Ziko was also with Sr. Ramirez.

"We have Ramirez in the room," Garret reports.

The officials move-in closer to see the camera footage. The men nod admissibly, glancing at one another.

Before Sr. Ramirez can spot the C-4 package sitting on the conference room table Garret taps the 'send button' on the phone. The receiver on the C-4 picks up the cell signal. And within a split second, the bomb detonates, cutting off Garret's camera view of the room. Knowing that Sr. Ramirez and his men were still in the room when it all went ***KA-BOOM***.

One of the officials turns to the Director: "we will have to confirm if the target was hit."

"Uh…" the Director raises his brow. He is surprised that the men want another confirmation. "Of course," he agrees.

He leads them to the computer monitor on the table that was receiving a satellite images from above the Hacienda. They glance questionably at Garret all the while they walked to the table. They probably wonder how he was able to come up with such invention.

Garret stands next to the Director as he clicks a few buttons on the keyboard. The aerial satellite image is shown on the computer screen. There's a thick mushroom cloud of smoke rising from what was once Sr. Ramirez' hideout. The men watch with awe across their faces.

Garret has his eyes on the screen as well. His countenance is clear. There's relief in his mind. He has finally avenged Barny's death. That is worth more than anything.

Also, he has proven to the officials that the B-system is arguably the deadliest invention since the atomic bomb. Nobody can hide from being assassinated and nothing is safe from destruction.

However, the full function of the system is not complete yet. Garret still needs to figure out how to teleport living organisms such as humans. Garret is confident with the funding of the C.I.A., and the construction of a new government lab he will have the most sophisticated equipment to work with. Even though Garret has earned an alley and the recognition of the United States Government he still feels somewhat uneasy with the government as his partner. Can the government be trusted?

BACK OF THE BOOK:

They say that Artificial Intelligence (A.I.) will be the destruction of mankind. The complete extermination of civilization... But what if one invention can have the same results? Even more devastating than A.I.!

What if someone invents the means of 'teleportation'? Beam Me Up in real life... No more planes to travel in, just teleport to place you want to go... another city, another state, to the mountains us to your favorite beach in Fiji, anywhere...No more cars to drive to the grocery store, your groceries would be teleported to you. Place your order and wham, there are your groceries sitting on the kitchen counter ready to be put away.

No more Federal Express or UPS or even the postal service. all packages and mail can be teleported to you. You can send your Christmas present to Grandma in Wichita in seconds. What devastation would ensue! 85% of the workforce would become unemployed. A complete collapse of the world system would create global chaos.

Think of the military use for teleportation? Bombs could be sent to the headquarters of world leaders. Assassins would be teleported to the offices or homes of targeted victims.

Garret Strong, Navel Scientist in Quantum Physics has discovered the means of teleportation. He holds the key to the most destructive invention mankind has ever developed. More devastating than knowing the codes to the atomic arsenal... and more powerful than all financial institution put together....

What will Garret do with his new invention and what will others do to try and steal his invention for personal gain and wealth beyond comprehension? One of the most sinister underworld drug lords wants Garrets invention along with the CIA, KGB and the Chinese.

Senior Rodriguez, the leader of the Sinaloa drug cartel, could ship tons and tons of drugs everyday around the world making him billions of dollars daily. His drugs would be undetected if he had Garrets teleportation system. The Russian's, Chinese and other foreign countries could use teleportation as military weapons and the use of global extortion. Currency confiscation of dirty money laundering would be a thing of the past.

Follow Garret from the beginning of his experimentations thru his trials and tribulations to the completion of the world's first teleportation system.